TALAR MOHAMMED

THE THINGS THAT APPEAR AT NIGHT...

novum pro

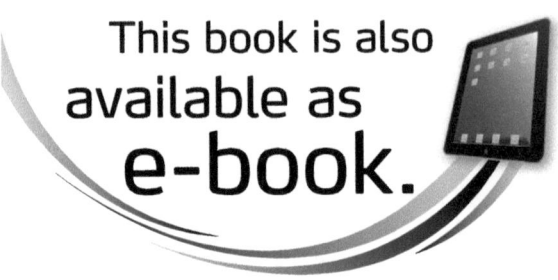

This book is also available as e-book.

www.novum-publishing.co.uk

ISBN 978-3-99146-095-4
Editing: Samantha Acker
Cover photos: Giovanni Triggiani,
Siarhei Nosyreu I Dreamstime.com
Cover design, layout & typesetting:
novum publishing
Internal illustrations: Talar Mohammed

The images provided by the author
have been printed in the highest
possible quality.

www.novum-publishing.co.uk

Print product with financial
climate contribution
ClimatePartner.com/16547-2311-1001

Contents

Chapter 8

CHAPTER 1

Purple Light?

I was trying hard not to doze off. I was in history class. Ms. Emily, my history teacher, has been talking for an hour now. She was explaining what all happened in World War 2. I really like history. It's interesting to know what all happened before I was born, how barbaric and inhuman people used to be. But having to listen to someone explain something for almost an hour is hard. So, I kept trying to stay awake and concentrate on what she was saying, in case she asks me a question unexpectedly. Teachers have a habit of doing that. I always get a panic attack when a teacher randomly asks me something; I then start stuttering and feel like the whole class is looking at me and judging my everything. It's like I can feel their judgy eyes, burning through my skin – even though it's not always the case. But, thanks to my overthinking mind, I can't help but think in that negative way.

I looked at the clock that was on the classroom wall, above the door. Just two more classes to go, biology and math. I have to survive a little longer.

After the classes were over, we got homework on every subject we had today, as if we didn't have anything better to do. Do the teachers really think we have no personal life other than school life?

I looked at my school schedule and saw that I still had two more hours of Physical Education (P.E.) before I could go home and rest. GREAT.

I hate sports. Not because I didn't like to exercise, but it was because we girls had to play with the boys, who played like they were in World War Three or something. We girls couldn't even have fun exercising. Since we were afraid one of the boys would accidentally hit us with one of the sports balls.

The boys kick and throw the balls so aggressively. I have always been a ball magnet. Everywhere I go, where people are playing with a sports ball, I somehow always end up getting hit by it. So, I stayed in a corner, praying that the time would go faster and that I could leave.

It was literally like a war field here; the chaos was overwhelming. I couldn't even hear myself think with all the boys shouting, running, and kicking balls everywhere. I looked over and saw that all the girls were standing somewhere in a corner, hoping not to get hit by the sports balls. *sigh* Yup, that's how we girls "exercise," every time we have gym class. We just stand somewhere and worriedly look around, in case we need to dodge a ball thrown or kicked by one of the wild boys.

I wish the P.E. teachers would finally realize that boys and girls aren't meant to play sports together ... especially now that we have become older. They should just split us up, so we could all have fun exercising safely. That way I didn't always need to make sure I survive, every time I have P.E. with these wild animals.

Oh well, I don't need to worry about this for too much longer. This was the last year of high school – just a couple more months and school ends. Then we would get our diploma and finally graduate. That is, if we work hard and pass our central exams.

Everyone in my class already knows what they want to become and have their life all planned out. As if it's the easiest decision you could ever make. This decision would have impact on our whole life. That frightened me the most and makes it hard for me to choose something. I still didn't know what to become and so I told my school mentor that I needed a gap year. That way I would still have time to decide what I genuinely want to become.

When the school day was finally over, I quickly cycled back home. It was already time for dinner. I helped my mom set up the table and ate dinner with my family. We had my favorite: lasagna! Yummy! Every bite I took made me feel like I'm in heaven. I felt the flavors melting on my tongue, making me forget everything that stressed me out today. I felt like Remy from *Ratatouille*, during the scene when he was tasting the cheese and the strawberry.

After we were done stuffing our faces, I and my brothers Danny and Ben, helped my mom with the chores. When I was done with my half of the chores, I went upstairs to my room to do all the boring homework I got today.

It took me 10 minutes to finish both my biology and history homework. Since they were two of my favorite subjects, but, for my math homework, I needed 40 minutes. Because I'm so terrible with numbers, shapes and whatever else has to do with math. I never understood what math had to offer me in life, other than agony and emotional breakdowns. I just hope I don't fail my central exams just because of math. I really needed to work hard if I wanted to graduate and not have to redo this year of school. I don't think I could survive another year of school.

After I was finally done, I went downstairs to watch a movie with my family. We were watching, *The Hobbit: An Unexpected Journey*. I would do anything to be able to go to a world full of magic and scary, yet fun, adventures.

A world where I could wander around carefreely and not worry about a thing. Especially not to have to worry about all the expectations my parents had for me. I know they only want the best for me, but sometimes it can be overwhelming. It's really hard trying to make them happy and proud of me all the time. Sometimes I do stuff only to make them happy, and I forget what delights me.

I saw how Bilbo and the dwarves were caught by the three trolls who wanted to eat them. This was one of my favorite scenes because it shows how useful Bilbo is, despite how small and weak he is. He always knows what to do and always ends up saving the dwarves.

I love the action and excitement of this movie. You can never get bored watching it; I have watched it over a hundred times already. Too bad I live in such a boring world and boring town, where nothing exciting ever happens. I never liked living in Chesterville. I have been living here since I was born. We somehow never needed to move away. When I turn eighteen, I would not hesitate to leave this boring place and go somewhere more crowded and alive, like a vital city.

When it got late, I went to bed, but I couldn't sleep, again. I guess worrying about my future and expectations so much gave me a lot of stress again. This is something I always have struggled with. Since I started being more responsible and have to make big decisions in my life.

My anxiety and fears really have an impact on my sleeping and my health.

When I stress about something, I always get really painful stomachaches. I even went to the doctor to check if anything's wrong with me. But every time I would go, they would tell me that my stress is so much that it quickly impacts my body and gives me painful cramps. They would then tell me to just calm down and relax. That's easier said than done, doc.

So, after it was twelve o'clock midnight, I was still awake and heard my parents brush their teeth. A couple of minutes passed by, and everyone was sound asleep, excluding me. I just couldn't go to sleep. So, I just laid on my bed looking at the white ceiling. I then started counting sheep in my head, that usually works.

Then suddenly, I saw a purple light reflecting in my room, through my windows. The light lit up my whole room; it was so beautiful. I got curious. I then got out of bed and walked to the windows to see what that was. I wasn't into sleeping anyway. So, when I walked up to my window, I saw a bright purple light in the dark starry sky. It kept coming closer.

First, I thought it was an airplane, but the purple object kept coming closer and closer, blinding me with its light. It then crashed in the middle of the woods, somewhere close to my house. It didn't make a lot of noise. I then started panicking. What am I supposed to do?

First, I thought I should wake my parents or call the police. This was an emergency. There could be people hurt or severely injured in that airplane. But then a random and crazy thought went through me and told me that I should go and check it out myself. It was in the middle of the night, so anything could happen to a girl like me. I was really scared, but my curiosity was much more powerful than my fear. Besides maybe a late-night walk would help me sleep.

So, I did the craziest thing ever, I quietly went downstairs put my jacket and shoes on, quietly opened the door and closed it carefully not to wake up my family. Then, I quickly sprinted over to the woods, like a careless idiot in a horror movie.

While I was walking through the dark woods, I had so many regrets. Why am I even doing this? This is madness! I should just call the cops so they can take care of it, but no, I am too stubborn to go back now. Especially since I have already come this far. So, I kept walking and, when I saw the purple light shining far from me, my heart was beating like crazy, as if I just ran a marathon or something. The smell of burned wood then filled my nose – a tree was on fire. I heard an owl howling somewhere in a tree. I felt like I was in a horror movie or something.

I then walked towards the light, something everyone says not to do, but I am an idiot, if you didn't know that. When I came close enough to the strange-looking airplane machine thingy, a wave of heat hit me. The heat came from the airplane machine thingy. I didn't know what it was, but I was sure it was not an airplane. So, I just stood there staring at it, trying to figure out what I was looking at. Then, in an instant, the strange machine thingy opened, and I saw a gray humanoid creature, who had big black eyes, strange shapes on his face, wavy short white hair, and strange pointy ears come out of the machine!

I couldn't believe my eyes. There was an alien creature looking right at me, and he was coming CLOSER!!!! OH MY GOD! What am I supposed to do? I don't want to get eaten! Oh no, I should have brought something to protect myself with. This was definitely not a good idea.

I slowly stepped back, and he kept coming closer to me, and he came so close to me, that we didn't have any personal space between us. He was three heads taller than me, which is not a real surprise, because I am truly short. He was of sturdy build. I bet he could overpower me without even trying. He looked right through me; I felt my body trembling in fear of what he might do to me.

I couldn't move or say anything, so I just stared at him. He stared back at me strangely like he's never seen a human being before. Of course he didn't; he's an alien after all, silly me. He then raised his right hand and put it on my head. I closed my eyes, ready to feel pain, but then the strangest thing happened. He took his hand away. I opened my eyes, looked at him, and he spoke to me in my own language! How is that even possible?!

He said, "Human girl, begone or else ... I WILL HURT YOU!!!"

Well, he did not have to tell me twice before I ran across the woods back home, went upstairs in my bed and pulled my blanket over my face, with my heart beating like crazy. After a couple of seconds, I slowly walked to my window and saw that he didn't follow me. Phew!" I sighed in relief. I got back in bed.

I couldn't believe it! I saw an ALIEN!!!! And he wasn't nice at all!!

I couldn't sleep. I kept thinking about that alien. "What was he doing there? What does he want? Where did he come from?" Those are the questions I kept thinking about, over and over again. I closed my eyes for a couple of hours and, before I knew it, my alarm went off. It was morning. My eyes were burning because of the lack of sleep I had tonight.

I quickly stood up, got myself ready and went to school as if nothing strange had happened. At school, I could not concentrate at all. I kept thinking about the alien. I really wanted to tell everyone what I saw but having a secret like this made me feel special and different in a fun way, and it somehow felt wrong to say, so I just shut my mouth.

I kept wondering what he was doing right now and why he came here in the first place. My friend kept talking to me, but I wasn't paying attention to her; I was lost in my thoughts.

So, when school was over, I quickly went back home, got a bag, put some food inside it and went back to the woods. I quietly went to the place where I first encountered him and saw that he was still there. He was busy with his spaceship.

I then breathed in and out, gathered some courage and said, "Hello."

He looked at me surprised, then he shouted, "What are you doing here!?! I thought I told you I was going to hurt you if you come close to me!!!"

I showed him the bag full of food and said, "I thought you might be hungry, so I brought you some food."

He looked at the bag and shouted, "LEAVE! I don't need help from a pathetic human like you!!"

My eyes started filling themselves with tears, and I felt like I was going to cry. So, I just dropped the bag there and ran as fast as I could back home.

My mom came to me and asked me what happened. I said, "Oh, it's nothing. I just got something in my eye. Nothing to worry about."

She looked at me trying to figure out if I was telling the truth. I then gave her a fake smile. She finally fell for it, nodded, and went back to the kitchen to keep an eye on the food she was making. Judging by the aroma of the food, she was making pasta with tomato sauce.

I then rushed to my room. OK, I do understand that sometimes people, or aliens, I guess, want to be left alone, but this kind of anger inside him was not normal. It was like ... I was like an enemy to him ...

The Next Day

At school, I was talking with my best friend, Anne. She has been my friend since kindergarten, and we both have brown hair and brown eyes. Sometimes people would assume that we're sisters. I wish we were. I always wanted to have a sister. We were talking about an anime series we both liked. So, yea, we are kind of *weebs*. The anime was called Maid-Sama. I love it so much! It's my favorite anime. Usually I tell Anne everything, and I wanted to tell her about the alien, since she and I are also fond of science-fiction stuff. But I somehow couldn't tell her. We always watch alien-related movies when we have sleepovers, and one time when we were still kids, we dressed ourselves as aliens on Halloween. Those were some good old memories; they were the times when we were too young to worry about our futures and everything else stressful that was to come. Sometimes I wish I could just go back to the time when I was still a carefree kid. My mind was so peaceful back then.

Anyway, it felt wrong to tell Anne for some reason. I preferred to keep it to myself in case she got too excited and told everyone. Since Anne does have a habit of not being able to keep a secret, so yeah, it's for the best, I guess. When school was over, I cycled back home, and ate dinner with my family. I wondered what my family would do if I told them about the alien. They would probably laugh at me and think I'm joking, since I always make stuff up to scare my little brothers for fun.

Then, I started wondering if the alien would be hungry too, so I put half of my food inside a lunch box, and then I went outside and cycled to the woods. I parked my bike next to a tree and went to the place where he had crashed. I saw his spaceship, but didn't see him, so I put the food next to his spaceship and left.

On the way home, I wondered if he ate the food, I gave him last time. It wasn't there so, hopefully, he ate everything. I then went home and headed to my room. I put my comfy baby Yoda pajamas on and watched some funny videos and then went to my Art account and posted some of my art. I may not be popular at school, but, on this social art app, where you can make and post your art at the same time. I am quite the popular person. A lot of people like my art, and I have a lot of online friends. Only on this app, I can be myself and have friends who fully understand me and can really relate to me. Too bad those people live on the other side of the planet.

The Next Day

I woke up and I saw that I was late for school! Damn it! My alarm clock didn't go off. I rushed and put my outdoor clothes on, brushed my teeth and put my books in my bag, I ran downstairs. That's when I realized I had a whole week off from school. "Phew!" I guess I forgot since my mind has been so busy thinking about that alien the whole time.

I went back upstairs and went in bed again, but it was too late; my parents were also awake. So, I had to come back downstairs, to eat breakfast. "Ugh!" I wanted to sleep in. So, I then came back down. After my mom made breakfast for all of us, we all sat down and started eating together. I am not a morning person so, I remained silent while my parents and brothers were all talking to each other. I then laid down on the couch and watched some TV. My favorite cooking program just started. I may not be a good cook, but I sure love to see others cook and get harshly criticized by the honest judges. When the program was over, I watched the news, and there was another person missing. During these past months, there have been a lot of people missing. The news keeps talking about how those people had disappeared unexpectedly. I can't believe that those people could just disappear without a trace, it's just not logical. I felt sorry for all their family and friends, who are worried sick. If there's one thing I know, it's that if someone is missing more than a month, they were most certainly killed by their kidnapper. I then turned off the TV. Too much sad and negative news can give you anxiety, and I have more than enough of that.

I then started wondering what that alien was doing. I wanted to know if he ate the food I gave him. So, I put a chocolate bar in my pocket and cycled to the woods. I saw him – he was busy with his spaceship.

Then, I gathered some courage again and greeted him. He looked at me with those big black eyes of his and said, "Why do you keep coming back, human girl? Don't you get that I will hurt you?"

I rolled my eyes and ignored him. I then pulled out the chocolate bar from my pocket, raised it in front of him and said, "This is called chocolate. You have to try it. It's really good."

He looked at me, clearly annoyed by me. He then looked at the chocolate bar and said, "If I take that from you, will you finally leave me alone?"

I smiled and said, "Yes." But that doesn't mean I'm going to leave him alone for real, because there's no way he is going to get rid of me that easily. Ha-Ha!

He then came closer to me and looked right into my eyes. It was like he was looking right through me. He then slowly took the chocolate bar from me and, as promised, I turned around and left him, only for today of course. I'm just glad he didn't shout at me again. I guess I'm making a little progress with him. When I was walking back toward my bike, I looked back and saw the bags that I brought for him the other times. They were empty now. So, he really did eat the foods I bring him. I then cycled back home with a big smile plastered on my face.

The Next Day

I was busy studying for a test in math, ugh! I had to take the test after the short holiday was over. While I was trying hard to understand the calculations I had to memorize for my test, my father called me from downstairs. I went downstairs to see what he wanted, and he then told me to get changed, because the whole family is going out. So, I rushed back upstairs and put some nice clothes on and went to wait inside the car. I guess I need to study some other time. Having fun with my family is more important now. I wanted to check on the alien and give him some food again, but I don't have time, and I bet he will be more than happy not seeing me for a day, *sigh* whatever …

We went to a park and had a barbecue with the entire family. I and my cousins wandered around the park. When we saw an ice cream truck, we obviously ran to buy some ice cream. I bought chocolate-flavored ice cream, and my cousins all got strawberry-flavored ice cream. I never understood how people could eat that flavor; it's so disgusting. Oh well, I guess everyone has their own taste, no matter how disgusting it may be to me.

We then found our special tree and climbed it. We always climb that tree when we come to this park, and we would talk about the weirdest and craziest things in our life. Of course, I didn't tell them about the alien incident. That's something between me and me alone. They don't need to know that. Some of them might even freak out and tell everyone.

I didn't know what it was about that alien but, I felt like I needed to help him. I felt like he was important somehow.

When it was time to go back home, it was almost nighttime. I looked at the sky and saw a beautiful full moon. I always wanted to travel the stars and be in space. I even considered becoming an astronaut once, but when I saw how hard it is to become one, I gave up. Apparently, you must be really intelligent to become an astronaut, and I, myself, am not the smartest person alive.

We rode back home, and, for a sec, I thought maybe I should check out what the alien is doing but, I was too tired. So, I just brushed my teeth and went to bed. It has been a long day. I bet the alien was also sleeping. Do aliens even sleep? Oh well, maybe I can ask him that tomorrow.

The Next Day

I got out of bed, ate breakfast with my family and did my chores. I then wandered around the house and realized that I have nothing to do, and I wasn't going to go anywhere with my family. So, I made some hamburgers, told my parents that I was going out for a walk outside and went straight to the woods to the alien.

Well, since I clearly have no life, I'm going to irritate an alien.

He was again remarkably busy with his spaceship. I keep wondering what he is doing, but I guess if I asked him, he would get mad and eat my brains, or is that a zombie thing? Oh well ... he saw me but didn't say anything. So I went to him and gave him a hamburger. He looked at me, slowly took it and said, "... How come you weren't here irritating me yesterday?" I replied, "Oh, that's because I was out with my family ... Why? Did you miss me?" I smirked. He looked at me with a poker face and didn't answer.

He then started eating the hamburger. I didn't know what to do or say, so I turned to leave, but then the alien said,

"Why are you leaving?" I turned around, surprised, and said, "Well, I thought you wanted to be left alone, so ..." He didn't say anything, and the tension was, too much. So, I quickly said something, "Oh, I was wondering what you're doing with your spaceship."

He said that his spaceship was wrecked after the crash and that he is trying to get in contact with other aliens, so that they can come and help him. I was surprised that he actually answered my question.

I felt a drop of water hit my skin. It unexpectedly started raining. I offered him to come back home with me until the rain stops, before he catches a cold – hmm, do aliens even get sick? I will ask him that later. First, he declined, but then it became worse, so he didn't have a choice but to come home with me. I had to make sure that my family doesn't see him. They would be shocked, and, besides, the alien doesn't seem to want to meet other humans, so yea.

When we got to my house, I peeked in the door's keyhole, and there I saw my whole family watching a movie. Good. This is my chance to bring him to my room. So, I rushed back outside and quietly brought him to my room and locked the door in case one of my annoying brothers barges in my room, like they always do. The alien was looking around. I gave him a towel to dry himself, and then I realized that I don't even know his name.

So, I said, "Hey, this might be a little too late, but what is actually your name?" He looked at me with those big black eyes of his and said, "You can address me with Atles." That is an unusual name, but I guess it must be a popular alien name from where he came from. He then said, "What can I address you with, human girl?" I also introduced myself and told him to sit down and rest till the rain stops. There was an alien in my room, who would have thought?

He was walking around my room and touching everything. Usually if someone else would do that I would get mad and

19

kick them out, but I guess he can be an exception. The rain didn't seem to stop sooner or later, so I offered him to stay the night and sleep in my bed. Surprisingly, he didn't deny it and nodded. So aliens do sleep, learned something new today. I then heard my mother calling me. I told Atles to stay in my room and to be quiet, while I go see what my mother needs me for. I left my room and to make sure he stays there I locked it and then went downstairs.

My mother told me to come and watch a movie with them, but I denied and lied to her that I didn't feel so good and that I am tired. So, luckily, she let me go. I brought some extra blankets and pillows from my parent's bedroom and went back to my room.

I then saw that Atlas was touching my precious action figure collection! Oh no, I quickly locked the door and put the blankets and pillows on the ground and ran up to him and nervously said, "'H-hey be-be careful, these are more important than my whole existence!!" He looked surprised and carefully put it back. I told him that it's getting really late and that we should sleep now. I offered him my bed and I went and slept on the floor. Great, I can't wait to wake up with a painful back. He was fast asleep and, before I fell asleep, I realized I forgot to brush my teeth. Damn it! … Oh well, I will do it in the morning.

Next Morning

When I woke up, I saw that Atles wasn't in my bed anymore! Oh no, I rushed downstairs and prayed that my family didn't see him. When I was downstairs my family was having a normal breakfast, my parents told me why I was in such a rush, I lied that I was just hungry that's all. Good they didn't see him. I quickly ate my breakfast, put some food inside my school bag, went back upstairs, put on some outdoor clothes, and told my mom I was going to go for a stroll outside. My mom said that she was glad that I have been going outside lately.

Usually, I just stay at home since I am too lazy to go anywhere. Ben looked at me and said, "Don't tell me you're going out so much because you finally got a boyfriend." He then started making kissing sounds. I lightly punched him and said, "Leave me alone, and mind your own business, you brat." He laughed and then went outside to play football with Danny, in the backyard. Those two are a handful sometimes. They always get in trouble at school. I am only grateful that they keep our parents attention to themselves, which gives me the perfect opportunity to keep Atles a secret.

I ran to the woods and, when I saw Atles busy with his spaceship, I was relieved. I then asked him when he left the house. He said the second the rain stopped, he went outside. I looked at my phone and saw that the rain stopped somewhere in the middle of the night. Good. No one could have seen him then. I hope not.

I gave him the food and said that he should be more careful; otherwise other humans could see him. He asked, "Why is that a problem? You are a human, and you act normal with me."

I told him that not all humans are the same. There are bad and good humans, and, if he doesn't be careful, the FBI or other governmental people will spot him and put him in Area 51 to experiment on him. He looked confused and said, "So, according to you, there are all kinds of humans on this planet. But how do I know if they're good or bad humans?"

I then said, "Trust me, no one knows each other 100%. Even we humans don't know that." He looked at me and said, "But, I know you are a good human." He then smiled at me and started to eat; I felt my cheeks warm up. I then said, "Well, yea, I guess so." That was the first time I saw him smile. He actually looked really cute. I then started getting a strange feeling I've never felt before.

I sat down and watched him as he was repairing his ship again; I sat there for hours, and it started to get dark. I then closed my eyes for a sec. I felt so tired I couldn't open them again ...

The Next Day

I woke up on my bed. I was really confused as to how I ended up here. I didn't remember coming home after being with Atles. Don't tell me he took another risk in coming here.

I went downstairs and saw my parents sitting on the couch watching TV, while my brothers were playing football in the backyard. I saw that they already finished breakfast. I guess I slept in.

My mom then questioned why I was gone for so long yesterday and why I went straight upstairs to bed without responding to them, when they called me. I quickly said that I wasn't feeling so good yesterday, so that's why I went right upstairs to bed. Luckily, she believed me and stopped with the questions. But she was a little mad that I didn't answer her yesterday. This was getting too risky. If I keep this up, they will soon find out about Atles. I had to think of something to make their attention be on my brothers and not me. I better be more careful then.

After what happened yesterday, I didn't really feel like going to Atles. I can't make my parents question me again why their only daughter, who doesn't go outside that often, suddenly loves to go outside for hours now. I went upstairs, drew some sketches, and posted them on my art account. After a couple of minutes, I got more than a hundred likes on it. It always makes me happy to see how much people like my drawings and sketches. Sometimes people like them so much, they want to buy one from me. I love sending them my art. When I was little, I never thought that one day people would really like my art and would even want to buy it from me. It's a great honor.

After a couple of hours, I got really bored in my room. So, I went downstairs to watch some TV. After seeing that there are no fun things on the TV, I couldn't help but wonder how Atles is doing. I then remembered that he brought me back home when I fell asleep. So, it would be rude to not thank him for that.

Therefore, I put some sandwiches, chocolate bars and some orange juice inside my backpack and told my parents that I would not come back so late this time. They then thought for a moment, and thankfully they agreed and let me go.

I ran outside through the woods, back to that spot he crashed on. There he was, still busy with his spaceship. I greeted him. He looked at me with a small smile and said, "I knew you would come." I felt my face heat up. I then quickly thanked him for bringing me back to my home yesterday. Then I took out the chocolate bar and said, "Here, I knew you loved it the last time you tasted it." He took it from me and thanked me. After looking at the spaceship, I asked if he needs materials to fix it. He said that he, indeed, needs material but doesn't know where to find it or if this planet even has the material he needs. I quickly told him to wait here. I then rushed back home and went to the kitchen. When I saw that my mom wasn't there, I quickly grabbed the mixing machine, the toaster and the coffee machine. I then went upstairs to my room and also took my hair dryer and a couple of old devices we never used. I put all of it in an old bag of mine and rushed back outside to Atles. When I stood in front of Atles, I was breathing heavily. I literally have no stamina. I really need to work out more. I then gave him the machines and said, "You can maybe use them to repair your ship with." He looked at them and smiled.

The Next Day

I hurriedly put some food inside my bag and ran to the woods to see how far Atles was since he now has some new material to fix his ship.

When I went back to the spot in the woods, I couldn't find any trace of him. I assumed he fixed his ship and left. I saw the print of where his spaceship crashed on. I felt my heart sink, and I then wondered why he didn't even come to say goodbye. After all, I was the one who helped him all this time, and wasn't I a friend to him? With those thoughts in my head, I returned home and went to my room knowing that I must go back to my normal boring life again.

I didn't eat and just stayed in my room drawing some sketches and posting them. My mother then started questioning about where all her kitchen machines were. I acted very innocent saying, "I don't know. Maybe someone stole them yesterday, when the front door was left open by Dad." Thankfully, she didn't suspect me and believed what I said. She then went and bought everything online, with my father's credit card. Sorry, Dad. Sometimes sacrifices must be made, for the greater good.

After it got dark, I went to sleep. It felt strange. It's like nothing ever happened. I'm just living my life again, just like I did before I met Atles. I then realized I didn't like that at all. I didn't want to go back to my normal life. I wanted to keep having a cool secret and an amazing friend. I can't believe how much I miss him, even though I had just seen him yesterday. That ungrateful idiot. I will never forgive him for leaving me without saying anything.

CHAPTER 2

Planet Komitaz

A couple of months came by. I went back to my normal routine of going to school and coming back home every day. The final exams also came along. I barely made it. I was really exhausted with all that studying I had to do. I was running behind in my studies and school, thanks to a certain 'friend,' but I'm sure glad I, at least, made it and miraculously passed my classes. And now that summer vacation started, I can finally rest out.

It was night, I was in my room drawing one of my favorite anime characters. I was drawing Katsuki Bakugo, from the anime called My Hero Academia. Suddenly I saw the purple light, shining in my room. My heart started to beat faster. I quickly looked outside through the window, and it was him. He came back!!!!

I rushed outside and there he was, standing in front of me, looking at me with his black eyes. I didn't know if I should be happy seeing him or mad that he left me without saying goodbye. He walked up to me, grabbed my hand, and told me to go with him because he needed to tell me something important. He looked more serious than usual, so I just nodded and went with him to his ship. I never saw the inside of his spaceship, so I was curious how it looked.

His ship was exceptionally clean, and the technology was so different and more advanced than what we humans have. Of course everything was purple. It looked amazing. He flew the ship somewhere above the clouds, so that no one would see the ship and freak out. He then looked at me and said,

"First of all, I was meaning to thank you for helping me all this time, and I apologize for leaving without saying anything. I just had to leave as soon as possible to my planet and tell them that I had not been captured." I didn't know what to say to him. I'm just glad to see him again, and I'm happy that he apologized.

Then I asked, "Is that the only reason you wanted to speak to me?"

He then said, "No, there is still something important I must tell you ... you know, before we came to this planet, we were told that you humans are all evil and needed to be destroyed. But when I met you, you were much different than what they have told us about humans: You are kind, thoughtful and really generous. Nothing like what we were told back on my planet. So that's why I want to help you ... You see, a long time ago we came here to study this planet and the inhabitants in it, but then you humans showed up and kidnapped a couple of us and put us in some kind of place in the middle of a desert. This angered our leader, so he planned to attack this planet and destroy you humans."

I was shocked, I didn't want to die!! So, I quickly said, "But not every human is evil. If he attacks this planet, he isn't only going to kill evil people, but also good people and innocent animals living on this planet!!!"

He told me that he knows that, and that's why he wants me to go talk to the leader and prove to him that not every human is the same, and I had to earn his trust for the sake of the human race. I agreed to do it even though I was freaking out. I know I keep saying that I want a more adventurous life, but this is insane!! I'm going to go to another planet full of aliens! I told Atles to wait so I could pack some stuff and tell my parents that I'm staying at someone else's house before they start panicking that I'm missing and all. Atles parked his ship in the woods and stayed there, waiting patiently, till I arrange things at home. I can't believe that its true about

Area 51, having aliens locked up. I thought it was all a conspiracy theory. This keeps getting weirder.

The Next Day

I fully packed my suitcase and went to talk to my parents. I told them that I'm going to go stay at my new friend's house, who was taking me to a faraway city to stay there and celebrate her birthday party. Surprisingly, they let me go and told me that they're happy that I'm finally socializing more with people, instead of staying in my room and drawing. If only they knew that I'm socializing with an alien; I'm pretty sure they wouldn't let me go. I then said my goodbyes to them, closed the door after me and I rushed to the woods and went in the spaceship. I had also brought a lot of snacks for the trip; in case I don't like the alien food. He started the ship and with such high speed, we were in space within seconds. I shared some food with him while looking through the window at Earth, which was slowly going out of sight. I missed it already, even though I have lived there since birth. It only took a couple of minutes, before we were there; the planet was green and much bigger than Earth and had rings just like Saturn After we landed there, I was getting nervous. These aliens all hate humans. What if they do something to me. Even though I was scared, I somehow trusted that Atles would protect me. When we were heading to the tall building where the leader is, everyone kept staring at me with faces full of surprise and disbelief. It was all getting a bit too much for me. I felt the sweat all over my body and felt my legs getting weaker. Atles then unexpectedly held my hand, and that support was exactly what I needed at that time. I felt more relaxed, thanks to him.

What surprised me the most was that this planet has oxygen just like Earth. Even though there are no trees to be found here, except strange-looking mountains with rock-like diamonds on them. The sky was green, and the rivers, coming from the mountains, were purple.

We then went in a strange room with the same purple lights just like Atles's ship. There were aliens surrounding us and, there, in the middle, was the leader. He was much bigger than the other aliens and had that scary look in his eyes, making my body shiver in fear. It got quiet in the room when they all saw us. Then the leader spoke in their own language to Atles, and Atles answered him. Probably telling him what I'm doing here. Then the leader looked at me and said, "Human girl, what is your name?" I answered, "M ... my name is Tayler Star, sir." He then said, "So ... you claim that humans are all different and that there are also good humans on Earth?" I then said, "Yes, that's true. There are a lot of good humans out there, and I understand that you're mad at humans, because of what they did to your people, but, if you attack Earth, you will also kill the innocent humans and animals who have nothing to do with anything that is happening." It was quiet for a moment, and then he said, "If you want to prove to us that there are also good humans on Earth, then go and save our kind from your people ... then I might spare your race."

I was terrified. How am I going to save the aliens that are locked up in Area 51? It's fully secured and full of military soldiers guarding it. How am I supposed to go past them. Without thinking it through, I quickly said, "OK, I will do it." All the aliens looked at me, surprised by my decision. Even the leader was shocked by my answer. He looked at me with wide open eyes. After some seconds, he then said, "The fate of your race is in your hands then, Tayler Star."

It's not like I had a choice, because, if I had said no, I bet they would have just killed me and then attacked Earth and killed everyone there. I may be scared, but I must be brave for my family, my friends and for the Earth.

I thought they would send me back to Earth right away, but they let me stay on the planet for some days to prepare myself for the upcoming mission. They even said that they're going to give me some weapons so that I wouldn't die immediately and have a better chance of succeeding.

Atles promised me he would help me and protect me. I'm really glad to have a friend to rely on in this particular complicated situation I have put myself in. They took me to a room to rest. I laid on the strange round bed, thinking and worrying about what would happen, if I fail this mission. I would die, and even if I don't die in the mission. I would get killed, when the aliens attack Earth.

Then someone knocked on the door. I quickly stood up and said, "Come in." The door opened, and an alien came inside and said, "Come with me." Without any questions, I followed, and he took me to an empty room. All he said was to stay here. Then he left and closed the door behind him. I felt my breathing speeding up, and my hands started getting a little shaky.

Then, out of nowhere, a table appeared with some gadgets on it. I wasn't sure what they were or how they were used, so I just tested them out. That was a bad choice. After I pushed a button on the bracelet-shaped gadget, it started shooting blasts nonstop. I panicked and threw it away from me. Luckily, it stopped shooting. I went back to the table and saw a gadget that looked like sunglasses, I wore them and looked around. They looked like ordinary sunglasses, but then I felt a button on the frame. I pushed the button, praying that it wouldn't go crazy like the bracelet thingy. After I pushed it, I could see through things, just like Superman could with his X-ray vision. SO COOL!!! When I looked around with them on, I saw that the alien leader, Atles and some other aliens were watching me from another room using invisible mirror.

Then I realized that I shouldn't play around and focus. This may be super cool, but Earth is counting on me to protect it. So, FOCUS, Tayler. This isn't a game.

I saw a ring on the table. I put that on, too, and pushed the only small button on it. But nothing happened. Before I went to push the button again, I looked at my reflection on the gray, reflecting walls, and I realized that I was invisible. OMG! THAT IS SOOO COOL!! It's like I have the ring of power from the *Lord of the Rings*. I've always wanted to have invisibility powers. My dream has come true.

I pushed the button of the ring to be visible again. Then, I grabbed the bracelet gun and wore that, too. It's like I have real superpowers. I got a feeling that this might not be so bad after all. Raiding Area 51 is something everyone always wanted to do. I never thought I would be the one having the biggest chance of doing it. I thought that the training was over but I realized that they were giving me time to test and figure out how the weapons worked. That means that the training is only beginning. For some reason, having these cool gadgets made me feel a bit braver, and I felt like I had more confidence. Ok you can do this Tayler Star, just stay focused.

Then, a couple of meteors were coming right at me out of nowhere. I quickly dodged them, but there were more coming. I couldn't dodge everything, so I pushed the button of the bracelet. It started shooting the blasts. I broke down some meteors with it after shooting down a couple of other meteors. I got used to using the bracelet, and it was easy. It's just like using a gun, even though I have never used a gun. I have only seen people use it in movies and video games.

The meteors kept coming, and I kept dodging and destroying them with my bracelet gun. Then, using my X-ray glasses, I saw the machine where all the meteors were coming from. So, I shot it one time with my bracelet gun, causing it to explode and stop. *sigh* That sure was exhausting. The room then repaired itself like nothing ever happened. A door opened, and there was Atles, waiting for me with a smile on his face. I walked up to him. He then said, "I'm proud of you. You managed to utilize these weapons so quickly ... not

even some of the Komitaz here can get used to them so fast."
I looked at him funny and said, "Komitaz?" Then he said, "Oh,
I forgot to tell you. You humans call us aliens, but we are ac-
tually called the Komitaz."

I headed to my room to rest. After lying on my bed for some
minutes, someone knocked on my door again. Seriously, did
I really have to do a test again?! I can barely walk. But, when
the door opened, it was the leader of the Komitaz. I stood up
immediately. He had a profoundly serious and scary aura.
He stared at me for a moment. Then he said, "Great job on
your little test. After you're perfectly prepared and got used
to using the Komitaz tech, then you and Atles will go back
to Earth, and you will save the locked-up Komitaz." I quickly replied, "If humans really are as evil as you say, then I prefer to be a Komitaz." The leader looked at me with his poker
face, processing what I had just said. And he then left without saying a word.

I realized that I've been here for a while, and it has still not
gotten dark. I figured that this planet stays daytime forever, which means I may have already been here for a couple of
days without knowing it. I will ask Atles about this later, just
to make sure. After a couple of hours drawing and making little sketches on my little sketch book, I got bored. Therefore,
I went outside to explore this strange planet. Before I left, I
put on new clean clothes, because the others had gotten dirty
during the test.

When I went outside, the Komitaz all still stared at me, but
I was too focused on the planet to get bothered by them. The
planet was gorgeous. It had a lot of strangely shaped mountains that had crystals on top of them. The planet was un-
like Earth: exceptionally clean and taken care of. If humans
knew about this planet with advanced technology, I bet they
would try to steal it and kidnap every Komitaz that lives here.
Just like they did to the homes of all those animals who are
all put in zoos for human entertainment. It's not that I don't

like zoos. But now that I notice how selfish humans can be and that those animals, just like the Komitaz here, all want to be free with their families. I realized that it's wrong. It makes me sad, and I feel disgusted of being a human.

It was lunch time. All the Komitaz went to the main building. They went inside a spacious room; it was a cafeteria. I didn't even know they had one. If I knew sooner, I wouldn't have eaten my Earth snacks that I brought here.

I went to the cafeteria and waited in line patiently until it was my turn. The food was totally different than what I was used to on Earth. I sat down and analyzed the strange looking purple food. Usually I'm a really picky eater, but I was hungry, and I can't keep eating my noodles, sweets and candy every day. So, I took a small bite. The second the food landed on my tongue, I spat everything out. I have never eaten something so disgusting. I then wiped my tongue with my hands till the horrible taste was not in my mouth anymore. I then looked around and noticed that everyone was looking at me and even the cook looked at me. I didn't want to be disrespectful, so I quickly just put everything in my mouth, swallowed it and did a thumbs-up to the cook. The cook looked away and went back to serving the food. I realized everyone was still staring at me. I quickly cleaned my table and left the cafeteria. Why do I always end up making a fool of myself in public? This is exactly the reason why I prefer to stay at home, where I can be free from those judgy eyes.

While I was walking through the halls of the building, I started wondering where Atles was. Ever since I did my test, he just vanished. I then wandered around the building looking for him.

I was deep in my thoughts but when I looked up I saw a big muscular Komitaz coming right at me. He looked angry and started yelling at me in his Komitaz language. I had no idea what he was saying and what he wanted from me. I tried to calm him down, but then he tightened his fist and right before he wanted to punch me, Atles showed up in front of me holding the crazy Komitaz's fist. The crazy Komitaz then said some other things I couldn't understand and left. I felt my body relax again; thank god Atles showed up at the right moment. I hugged him and thanked him for saving me.

He looked away and said, "You should be more careful. I told you that all the Komitaz hate the humans." I asked him what that crazy big Komitaz wanted from me. He said, "Well, his little daughter was also captured by the humans, and that's why he wanted to throw his anger all to you ... because you're also a human."

Even though it wasn't right to attack me all of a sudden, I still felt sorry for him. Atles brought me to his room. I found it a bit weird that he lives in the large building instead of having his own house, just like most Komitaz I saw outside. After I asked him, he told me that only if he marries someone, he must leave the nest and make his own house. Then without thinking what I was saying, I asked, "Well, how come you're not married? You're handsome, polite, and strong." I immediately regretted saying that. It was weird telling him that out loud. I felt my heart beating faster and felt my face flush. I noticed that he was smiling. So, I then quickly broke the ice and said, "Well, anyway, it's been a long day, so I think I'm going to go to sleep now. I bet I will need as much energy as possible for my other tests!" He nodded and took me to my room, just to make sure I got back safely. I was fast asleep thanks to the fluffy round purple bed.

The Next Day

I woke up, put some flexible clothes on, so I could move easier for my next test. After I went to the cafeteria to have breakfast, I wasn't surprised that the food was disgusting again. The food looked like pudding, but it was slimier, and it smelled bad; I had no choice but to eat it. I needed the energy. No wonder Atles really liked the food I kept bringing him back on Earth. Anything is better than what they have here. I went back to the room where I did the test last time. This time, I had to practice hiding and being quiet by using my invisible ring. This way, I would easily raid Area 51 without anyone noticing. Good thing I was good at hiding and being quiet. I easily passed the test. I then went back to my room to rest a bit. I thought about my family. I hope they don't try and call me. There is no signal here. I bet my parents have their hands full with my wild brothers, who always end up making trouble for our poor tired parents.

Then it was lunchtime again. Usually, I can't wait to eat but, on this planet, I prefer to starve. I took my bag full of food with me this time and went to the cafeteria. I didn't take any food from the cook, instead I sat down on one of the tables and brought out some Earth food.

I got out my little cooker and warmed up some noodles. Then, I took out a lot of chocolate bars and bread with soup. All the Komitaz there smelled the delicious aroma of my food and looked at me and my food. I figured that if I want the Komitaz to like humans, I better give them some human-made food, just like I did with Atles. They all just looked at me, so I went to the cook and gave him a cup with noodles and told him to try it. After he ate some, he happily yelled something in their language. He probably said that it was the most delicious thing he's ever eaten. Soon the other Komitaz surrounded me, all wanting to taste Earth food, too. Good thing I brought a lot of food with me. I gave them all a snack. They were all happily eating it. That's when the Komitaz leader appeared at the doorframe. I went to him and gave him a chocolate bar, but he didn't take it, so I just grabbed his hand and put the bar in his hand and said, "Just try it. You won't regret it." He looked at me without saying anything, turned around and left. What a grumpy old Komitaz.

I saved some chocolate for Atles and myself and headed back to his room. He wasn't there, so I looked around his room and found a tablet. I didn't want to go through his private stuff, but I just couldn't help myself. I had to know what he had on his tablet. Back on Earth, I saw him typing things on it sometimes. But before I could look through his tablet, the door opened – it was Atles. I quickly put the tablet back where I found it. He came to me and asked me what I was doing here. I told him that I saved some chocolate for him after sharing the other snacks with some Komitaz in the cafeteria.

He said, "Thank you, Tayler Star, and I'm happy that you managed to show your good side to the other Komitaz, but don't go to close to them. It's still risky. Some of them might do something to you, and I won't be around to help ... understand?" I was happy that he cared about me, but it's almost like he is jealous that I'm being nice to other Komitaz. Even though the only reason I'm here is to prove that there are also good humans. So, I said, "But, am I not supposed to prove myself to them. Isn't that the reason why I'm here?" Then he shouted, "NO! You are here to train and prove yourself by saving the others on Planet Earth, not by being nice and getting close to other Komitaz here!" I got startled by his sudden outburst, and I felt a bit scared of him. He acted just like he did when we first met. I almost forgot how scary he can be.

But when he noticed my scared face, he quickly apologized and said, "I just don't want something to happen, just like with that other crazy Komitaz who attacked you." I told him that he doesn't need to worry and that I already have everything under control now. I also said, "Even if something like that happens again, I'm pretty sure you will save me again, as my hero." I smiled and winked at him. He then calmed down and smiled at me and said that he would try his best to protect me.

After chatting with him about the planet for some time, I went back to my room. I took out my little sketchbook and started drawing random things while sitting on the floor. I then started making a quick little sketch of Atles in my own art style. My eyelids then started getting really heavy – until I couldn't open my eyes anymore. ...

The Next Day

When I woke up, I realized that I was on my bed. I wondered how I got here if I fell asleep on the floor. Even my sketchbook and pencils were put in my little bag. I had a feeling Atles came in my room and did this, just like he did when I fell asleep in the woods, when he took me back to my room. I bet he even saw the sketch I made of him. I hope he didn't see it; that would be so embarrassing. Then again, he really is sweet for taking care of me like this.

I took a bath in the little bathroom inside my room. Atles had told me that I could wash myself in the little tub filled with purple water, after I asked him where I could wash myself. I came out of the little tub, feeling refreshed and clean. Too bad the purple water was freezing. I guess the Komitaz don't have warm water. I then put some clean clothes on and headed out to do my next test. When I went to the training room, I had to learn how to use the bracelet gun. I had to destroy the fake humans. The fake humans were guarding a plush toy, who represented the Komitaz locked in Area 51.

I did the test, but after I was done, I went to see the leader and the other Komitaz, together with Atles, who were in the room watching me practice. I then said, "I want to save the Komitaz on Earth and prevent Earth from being attacked by your kind ... but I will not kill anyone." They all talked to each other in their own language and then faced me. The leader then said, "Very well, we're going to make you another weapon that doesn't kill. Anyway, you're doing well in your training. After a couple more tests, you will go back to Earth and prove yourself to us." I was glad they were giving me less harmful weapons. Then a random Komitaz came to me and complimented me on my tests. I thanked him and smiled. He was shorter than Atles and had wavy white hair. Then I noticed Atles, looking at me with a poker face. I didn't understand what was going through his head. I ignored him and chatted with the other Komitaz, who were all surrounding me and questioning me about Planet Earth. I happily explained to them how it is on Earth and how different it is than this planet. They were all listening to me, which made me a bit nervous. I then felt my cheeks warm up. That's when the Komitaz around me started touching my cheeks in curiosity. I guess they never saw a human blush before. Then Atles came to me and, using a head gesture, he told the others to leave. They all left, and then I said, "Why did you scare them off? They weren't threatening me or anything." He said nothing and just looked at me with his big black eyes. It was like he wanted to say something to me but couldn't say it and wanted me to just notice it instead. I really wanted to know what was going on in his mind, instead of giving me such a tough time. It's hard trying to understand him and to see through his poker face. The Komitaz don't show a lot of facial expressions, making it hard to understand how they feel.

It was finally lunchtime; I went to the cafeteria with Atles and ate lunch with him. I was really getting used to the food here. I ate it all up without trying to not throw up. Atles chuckled and said, "I know the food doesn't taste good. This food is made of the purple materials on the mountains of this planet. Everything we have is made with the purple materials: our food, clothes, houses, oxygen, and, most importantly, our high technology. We call the purple material, 'Ikvi.'" He told me a lot more stuff about his home planet. Apparently, Planet Komitaz doesn't have any animals or other creatures living on it, and there are also no trees or plants. The Ikvi that grows on the mountains and inside the caves of this planet makes life possible for the Komitaz.

There is so much to learn about this planet. Too bad I don't have much time to do that, since I have to train and get ready to save the Komitaz and save Earth from the war against the mighty Komitaz race. I kept wondering what would have happened if I had never met Atles. I was wondering what would have happened if our meeting never took place. Earth would then suddenly get attacked by the Komitaz race, and I would never know what the cause was. I started biting my nails, while being lost in my thoughts.

Atles grabbed my hand after seeing me getting a little anxious. He then took me to his room. I asked him what he wanted from me, he said, "Just stay here, and let's talk together. It's been a while since we spend time with each other." I didn't know how to respond to that, so I just did what he asked and started talking about the mission.

He then told me to forget about all that and talk about something else, so he said, "Did you pass the central exams at school?" I said, "Yea, I barely made it, but I passed, and now I don't need to stress anymore for school or anything … well, that is until all of this happened." He then apologized for all this trouble, I had to go through, even though it has nothing to do with me. I said, "It's OK. I'm actually enjoying it. I'm grateful I got to meet you and be here on your planet, trying out cool weapons and all." I smiled at him, and he gently smiled back at me.

Before we could talk more, the Komitaz leader came in the room and disrupted our chat. I stood up and asked him, "So, how did you like the chocolate bar I gave you. It's one of Earth's special and most popular delicacies." He said, "It wasn't that bad, but don't think you can change my mind with some Earth food." I looked at him in disbelief and said that I didn't want to change his mind, but that it was just a little present. He ignored my comment and told me to go back to my room and rest until my next training session. He sure is grumpy. I feel bad for the Komitaz, who must deal with him every day. I did what he asked and left the room. The leader stayed in Atles's room and talked with him about something. I wonder what they discussed that I wasn't allowed to hear.

The Next Day

I was in the cafeteria eating breakfast. When I was done, I went to the training room for my next training session. This time, they gave me a gun-shaped weapon, where it shoots only electric shocks. If I used this on someone, it would keep the person unconscious for only a couple of hours. "Phew!" I'm glad I don't need to kill anyone anymore.

This time, the test was awfully hard. I had to use all my gadgets and try to take the plush toy from robots, who even attacked me with Earth guns. I passed the test after almost dying. I thought I had other tests, but it was the final test. That means I'm finally done. I was relieved that all the tests were finished, but I was also really terrified that I had to do the real thing now.

Just when I went to my room to pack my stuff Atles, barged in my room without knocking and said, "Pack all your stuff. We're leaving in about ten minutes." He then quickly left. I hurriedly packed all my stuff.

I put everything back in my suitcase and was on my way to go to the ship. Then, that big and crazy Komitaz, who attacked me the other day, came right at me. I looked around to see if Atles was around to help me out this mess again, but, to my surprise, the crazy Komitaz calmly looked at me and said in my language, "Please, human, the only thing I want is to get my little girl back. Please save her, human girl." I felt bad for him, so I said, "Don't worry, sir, I have trained as hard as I could. I promise I'm going to bring your daughter back to you safely, uh, mister...?" He then said, "Maver. My name is Maver, and I apologize for the other time. I just miss my little girl so much I couldn't control myself when I saw a human." I told him that's it's OK and that I understand. After that, I quickly went inside Atles's ship. We went back to Earth at high speed.

Before I knew it, we were there again. Home sweet home. I never thought I was going to miss my home so much. But we aren't going home now. We must go to Area 51. Atles used camouflage for the ship, so that no one would see the spaceship and cause unwanted attention.

We were right above Area 51. I never believed that I was going to be the one raiding Area 51. I am so excited, but also extremely nervous. I should really concentrate. I'm here to save all the Komitaz that were abducted. I armed myself with all the weapons that were given to me.

Then, I said to Atles, "Come on, let's go and save all the Komitaz." But Atles said, "I'm sorry, I wish I could but, our leader clearly ordered me to stay on the ship, while you save the others because he doesn't want any more of us to be in danger." My heart dropped, and I felt my body getting heavy. All this time, I thought that he was going to help me. That's why I kept feeling less scared. And now that I really had to do it myself, I felt the pressure, really hard. Atles saw my scared face and said, "But if you want, I will ignore his orders and help you anyway." I then remembered what Maver told me and what the leader told me about proving myself. I then said, "No, that will only prove that humans aren't willing to risk their lives for others in need. I'm going to go alone and prove to everyone that humans can be good." Atles looked at me with a worried look. We stared in each other's eyes for some seconds, but it felt like hours. It was like the time had stopped at that moment.

Atles then looked away and said, "OK, but please be careful, and take this with you. You might need to use it." It was the bracelet gun that could destroy anything. If I use this dangerous weapon, I could kill someone with it. I took it and wore it on my left hand. I hope I don't need to use it; I don't think I could ever kill someone. He opened the door. I pushed the button on my ring and turned myself invisible.

I then jumped out of the ship and landed in front of the gate of Area 51. I easily snuck past two soldiers guarding the front gate who were chatting with each other. They were talking about getting a drink after their shift was over. Right when I thought that this was going to be easy, I saw more than a hundred military soldiers, who were surrounding all of Area 51. It's like they knew I was coming. This is crazy. I may sneak in and out unnoticed, but what about all those Komitaz? They don't have the invisibility ring like me. How am I supposed to sneak out a bunch of Komitaz unnoticed with all those security cameras and military soldiers!?

I decided that I would think of a plan when I find them. I waited till someone would open the door so that I could go inside the building. Finally, a couple of scientists in white lab coats showed up and opened the door with their keycard. I quickly followed behind them inside.

When I was inside, I thought I would see those labs full of other aliens and mutants like in the movies. But all I saw was more than a million frightening weapons, like the nuclear bombs America used to destroy whole cities. I felt my heart beating so hard, it started to hurt. One small mistake, and I could activate one of those bombs. I kept my distance from the dangerous things and looked around. Without even noticing, I lost concentration and was wandering around looking at everything. It's not every day you get to break into Area 51. Everywhere I looked, there were guns, bombs. All kinds of deadly weapons. If they use these things at war or something, I bet they could just rule the entire world with it. I had to do something about this, but what? I could destroy everything after I get the Komitaz all out of here.

A group of scientists came in the room. I almost forgot that I was invisible; I nearly had a heart attack. I quietly listened to what they were saying. They were talking about how to make a weapon so powerful that not just Earth but even the planet of Komitaz should bow down to them. They needed the abducted Komitaz to help them build it.

I couldn't believe it, not only my planet, but also Atles's planet is at stake. I need to concentrate and save the Komitaz from here as soon as possible. I quietly left the room and started looking from room to room. I saw a lot of cool and dangerous stuff, but no sign of Komitaz. I can't find them alone. I went back to the room where the scientists were. Then I heard one of the scientists talking about going to interrogate one of the Komitaz. Perfect! I then quietly followed him to a room, which was fully secured. He led me to a spacious dark room. I then saw one of the Komitaz. He was tightly chained up and looked really exhausted. I saw scars all over his body. I felt bad for him. These people are so cruel for doing this. The anger started growing in me. I can't believe there are people who would do this kind of stuff.

The scientist started talking with the Komitaz about working together, but the Komitaz didn't say a word. Then, the scientist pushed a button on his tablet, and the Komitaz got electrified. I could almost feel how he suffered only by looking at his eyes. The Komitaz didn't scream or shout; he only looked at the scientist with anger and pain in his eyes. I couldn't take it anymore, so I ran up to the scientist and shocked him with electricity from my electric gun. He then lost consciousness. Then I quickly turned off the machine that was hurting the Komitaz and turned myself visible again.

The Komitaz looked at me with a surprised look. I quickly unchained him, helped him up and said, "Don't worry. You can trust me. I'm with you guys. I'm here to bring all of you home." He looked at me with confusion in his face and said, "Why is a human like you betraying your own kind and saving me?" I quickly said, "Even if they are humans like me, I can't stand seeing these people make others suffer for their own selfish purposes." I then asked him if he knew where the others were. He said that he didn't know because they kept being put in different rooms. I held his hand and said, "OK. Stay close to me. We're going to go find and save the other Komitaz here, too, and then we will finally escape this terrible place."

I heard some soldiers coming this way. I and the Komitaz went and hid behind a nearby door. We didn't have much time before someone would notice the scientist laying on the ground. After the soldiers were out of sight, we ran to another hall. I used my X-ray vision glasses to look through the rooms. While I was looking around for the others, the Komitaz then said, "Thank you for saving us. My name is Aton." I told him, "Don't thank me now because I haven't really saved you yet, and you can call me Tayler." He smiled at me and held my hand tighter making me blush a little.

After some time, I finally found them! They were all being held in one room. After the coast was clear, we went in front of the door, it was locked obviously. I then got out my electric gun and electrified the device that locked the door, and it surprisingly worked. The door unlocked and opened. We went inside, and there they all were – all the Komitaz that were ever abducted by humans. I and Aton unchained everyone. Aton then explained to everyone that I was here to save them. When I looked at all of them, there were five, all males, though. I realized I didn't see Maver's daughter here. So, I asked Aton, "Where is the little Komitaz girl? There should be a little girl here." He said that they must have brought her somewhere else. It was impossible to go and save her, too, with all these Komitaz with me. We would be caught in no time. I couldn't risk six Komitaz lives and my own life for one being. I decided I would save her another day. First, I needed to save these Komitaz.

Before we left the room, I looked with my X-ray glasses to see if the coast was clear. After there were no more soldiers and scientists around, we all headed to the front door.

I then saw all these military soldiers outside blocking our way out. They knew we wanted to escape. Suddenly, there was a loud siren. It was obviously the scientist who I electrified when I saved Aton. The scientist must have set the alarm and warned everyone of this rescue mission.

I didn't want to do this, but I had no choice. I told the Komitaz with me to all hold hands and not let go until we are safe. We formed a line with me in the front. I held Aton's hand, and I said, "Don't let go, and stay behind me. This is going to get really dangerous." Then I raised my bracelet gun, aimed it at the front door and shot the front door open. The military soldiers all started to shoot at us. I quickly stood in front of the Komitaz to protect them. Then, out of nowhere, I felt a searing pain I have never felt before. When I looked at where the pain was coming from, it was my arm. I was shot! My breathing quickened, and I felt the tears coming out.

Even though the pain was too much for me, I tried to ignore it. I got angry and started shooting every soldier I saw. The blasts were so powerful that I only needed to shoot a couple of times to take down a whole bunch of soldiers. I kept running with the Komitaz behind me. It didn't take long when I saw Atles appearing with his ship in front of us. He opened the door of his ship, and all the Komitaz quickly went inside. Before I went inside, I realized that there is still one Komitaz left, the little girl. Even though I was in a lot of pain, I just had to hold myself to the promise I made with Maver. Atles came to me worried because of my wound. I then told him to take the others to safety because I'm not done with my mission yet. I ran back before Atles could protest. I went back to the building; on my way, I saw a lot of dead bodies. I didn't want it to go this far, but the second they started shooting, I had no choice but to shoot back and protect myself and the innocent Komitaz.

I went back inside and looked through every room, but I just couldn't find the little Komitaz girl. I heard a couple of men coming from behind me. I quickly turned around and aimed my bracelet gun at them and shouted, "I will kill you if you come closer!" They were scientists, there were two of them. They then both started begging to be spared. I told them that I would spare them if they showed me where the little Komitaz girl was. They quickly agreed to show me. While I walked behind them with my bracelet gun aimed at them, they finally stopped in front of a door. To make sure they weren't lying to me, I used my X-ray vision glasses, and yes, there she was. I sighed in relief. I let them go and told them to leave without turning back or else I would end their life without showing any mercy. After they were out of sight, I went inside the room. I saw that she was put inside a cage. She also looked exhausted. They probably hurt her too with those inhuman machines. I looked for the key to open the cage. When I finally found it, I quickly opened the cage, unlocked the chains on her and told her not to worry and that I'm here to bring her back home to her father. She didn't say anything but it looked like she was scared of me. I wouldn't judge her after what she had to go through here. I then carried her in my arms, even though my arm still hurts. I then ran as fast as I could to the front door to escape, but then a scientist came in front of me and blocked the way. He said, "Hand that alien over immediately. I already called the full force to come this way, you will not escape as long as I'm here."

I was fed up with all of this, I was in pain, and I needed to save this girl, so I did something the old Tayler would never even think of doing. I aimed the bracelet gun at the scientist, told the little Komitaz girl to close her eyes and shot the scientist through his chest without showing any mercy. He fell over and started bleeding out. I heard helicopters and tanks from far away coming this way, so I had to be quick. I remembered that there are security cameras and, even with these glasses, people would recognize me, and this place is filled with dangerous stuff, so with the little Komitaz girl still in my arms, I went inside the room with the weapons and nuclear bombs. I quickly took out the largest nuclear bomb I could find and turned it on. According to the bomb's timer, I have 30 seconds to escape before everything explodes, so I ran as fast as I could away from the building. Before the military soldiers and helicopter came, the whole place exploded and got destroyed. It was like there was never an Area 51 in the first place.

Finally, after walking for some time in the desert, Atles showed up. He then landed right in front of us. I put down the little girl, who ran inside the ship, happy that she's saved and is finally going back home. But when I wanted to get inside the ship, I felt really dizzy. I looked at my arm and saw that I lost a lot of blood. I collapsed and, just when I thought I would hit the hard ground, I felt a pair of strong arms grab me and lift me up in bridal style, then everything went black ...

When I woke up, I was back inside my room on Planet Komitaz. I looked at my arm, it was bandaged nicely. Did that really happen? Oh my god! I just can't believe that I did all that. It feels like it was all a dream. Then, someone knocked on the door. I told them to come in, and it was the little girl together with her father, Maver. They came in happily and thanked me for everything. I told them that it was nothing, even though I almost died. Then, Atles came in the room. Maver and the little girl thanked me again and happily left the room.

Atles sat next to me on the bed and told me how proud he was and how worried he was when I blacked out. I didn't remember what happened next, so I asked him about it. He then said that he carried me inside the ship and let one of the others fly the ship, while I was drooling on his chest the whole time, on the way back. I was really embarrassed and apologized. He laughed and said, "It's OK, I thought you were cute in my arms like that." I felt my face heat up, while he kept staring at me with his black eyes. He gently smiled and said, "I like the color your face makes when you're shy. We Komitaz can't change our color, despite the different emotions we feel – not like you humans." I wanted to ask about that, but then there was knocking on my door again. I shouted out that they could come in. The door then opened, and Aton came inside the room, thanking me for saving them. He then sat next to me on the bed and held my hands. Suddenly, Atles annoyedly said, "Tayler needs her rest, so maybe you should go now." But then Aton replied, "Why should I leave? You are here, too, so why don't you leave instead?" They both looked at each other with dead serious eyes, like they wanted to kill each other or something. Then Atles said, "I've known Tayler before you did, so I think she would feel more comfortable being with me than being with you." Then before Aton got to say something else to Atles, someone else knocked on the door. When the door opened, it was the Komitaz leader. Aton and Atles quickly stood up, out of respect. The leader came to me and smiled at me and said, "You have proven yourself more than enough. I am truly thankful of your bravery that saved my people." I smiled and said, "It was nothing. I am happy that everything turned out OK." He then told me to change and come outside.

They all left, so I quickly changed and went outside where I saw the whole Komitaz race cheering for me. They all thanked me, and they even called me their heroine. The leader came next to me and said, "Today, we are here to thank our heroine who saved the missing Komitaz from Earth. She proved to us that in Earth there are good and bad people, and so ... I declare that we will spare Planet Earth." Everyone happily cheered. Then, the leader looked at me and said, "What can we offer you to show our gratitude to you?" I then said, "Well, I don't want anything, but if you could let me keep the cool gadgets you gave me, I would also be really happy." I grinned at him. Then, after thinking for a while, he said, "Well, if you really like those kinds of things, let us make you some new gadgets that are more flexible to use with smarter Komitaz technology." I thanked him and couldn't wait to get my new gadgets.

After a huge feast, I went back to my room to rest. I lost too much blood, so I kept feeling dizzy from time to time. I never thought that I, the girl who once was afraid of the littlest things, could do this and survive a real gun shot. I felt proud of myself. I wish I could tell my parents and make them proud of me, but I bet if I did tell them what I did, they would only scold me and never let me go outside again. They might not even believe me.

The Next Day

I woke up and I saw that someone was staring at me. I screamed at the top of my lungs and closed my eyes. But, when I looked again, I saw that it was Aton, so I said, "Oh, it's you, Aton, uh … What are you doing here … in my room, if I may ask?" He then said, "Sorry to have startled you. I just wanted to see if you're doing OK." Then I said, "Oh, you did more than startle me. Anyway, it's nice that you're worried about me, but, as you can see, I'm fine." He looked at me with a cute little smile, held my hand and said, "I'm glad to hear that my heroine is doing well. So, do you want to go have breakfast together?" Before I could reply, Atles came in the room, looked at us, turned to Aton and said, "What are you doing here?" Then that strange tension came back between these two. Aton then replied, "Well, I was just worried about Tayler, so I wanted to check on her. And, if you will excuse us, we were having an important conversation." I wouldn't say that this was important. He only asked to get some lunch together. But Atles looked at him with his cold, scary black eyes. Before I could say anything, Aton said, "I'm sorry Tayler Star, but because of some annoying circumstances, I think we should eat together some other time." Then he quickly left the room. I wouldn't blame him for running off like that. Atles can sometimes be scary, especially with those muscles and how tall he is. Then Atles sat next to me on the bed. I asked him why he came here. He replied, "Well, I heard your scream and wanted to check if you were OK, and I hope you weren't disturbed by that idiot." I said, "Well, not really. He was just trying to be nice to me, that's all." Atles then said, "Well, that's because you saved him. Otherwise, he wouldn't even look you in the eyes." I don't know where all of this was heading, but I replied, "Well, if I weren't so nice with you back on Earth by giving you food and all, I bet you wouldn't even care about me, so ..." That got him on edge. I then said, "Hey, I'm just messing with you." He helped me up, and we then headed to the cafeteria to eat. The food tasted much different. It was still disgusting, but at the same time, there was a little improvement in it. I guess I have gotten used to it. While I was thinking, I noticed Atles looking at me. I then said, "What's up?" He asked me to go for a walk and show me some more of the planet. I happily accepted the offer. I then quickly ate all the food and went outside with him. I was so glad I could explore more of the planet before leaving.

The Komitaz all still stared at me, but this time with a smile. Normally, I hate going somewhere else that's not my home, but for some reason I felt at home here. Atles took me to a purple waterfall. I went and tasted the water, and it tasted just like Earth water, but much fresher and cleaner, because on this planet there are no sea creatures or bacteria living in the water. So, the water doesn't need to be cleaned. If I knew how fresh the water here tasted, I wouldn't have brought so many water bottles with me.

Then, Atles carried me bridal style and flew me on top of a mountain to see the view better. He put me down. I then looked at the beautiful view. The planet looked much more peaceful now that everyone is back home. Just when I wanted to turn around, I slipped and almost fell, but Atles caught me just in time. He said, "Watch your step. The Ikvi on the mountains are very slippery." *Sigh* Couldn't he have told me that a bit sooner? I smiled at him and said, "Thanks." Even though I had my balance back, he hadn't let go of my hand.

I had that same strange feeling like when we were on Earth, when he smiled at me for the first time. My heart started beating faster. Why is this happening? He is an Komitaz, and I'm a human. This would never even work. Then, he looked at me and said, "Is everything OK? You seem a little nervous. Is it because I'm holding your hand? I can let go if you want." I quickly panicked and said, "What? No! I mean yes! But no! I'm just *sigh*... I don't know." I mentally faced palmed. He laughed and said, "This is the first time I've seen you get startled like that. I like the new emotions you are showing me." He smiled at me and held my hand tighter. I felt my face heat up. I tried to focus on something else. Why does he always manage to make me feel so nervous? Normally, I haven't had this kind of contact with boys at school or somewhere else. When it comes to dating or having crushes, count me out. Those kinds of things are not for me. No one has ever made me feel attracted to them. So, I don't really understand these kinds of things; this is very new for me. So, I'm kind of freaking out.

After a couple of hours wandering around and looking at the beautiful planet and feeling the nice warm wind on my face, we headed back to the main building, while still holding hands. I felt so peaceful. I wish it could always be so peaceful and safe.

The Next Day

I packed all my stuff to leave. Then someone knocked on my door. It was the Komitaz who brought me to the training room when I first came here. He told me to come with him. I then followed him, and he brought me to the room I trained in. But when I went inside, I saw the Komitaz leader and Atles waiting there for me with a bunch of other Komitaz behind them. The leader then said, "Ah, there you are. We have made you the new gadgets you wanted."

On the table, there were much better and upgraded gadgets. I picked up the invisibility ring, but it didn't have a button on it. Then, the leader said, "These gadgets are made of the newest and most intelligent Komitaz technology. This time, you don't need to push a button so that the devices do their thing. This time, the devices can study your emotions and thoughts. For example, if you're in a dangerous situation, this ring will sense that you want to be invisible and automatically you will become invisible." I put the ring on and hoped to be invisible and looked at my reflection, and it worked!! This is so cool. It's like I really have the power of invisibility! I only needed to think about it, and I was invisible. I picked up the bracelet and put that on, too. Then, Atles said, "With this device, we can contact each other, and you can use it as the thing you use on Earth named Google, but this doesn't need Wi-Fi. It is made of Komitaz technology, so it runs itself." Wow, that was so cool! I could also use it at tests to get all the answers right. Heh heh.

I looked at the table and found a pair of shoe soles. Then, Atles explained that, with those soles, I could put them on every shoe I wear and be able to fly with them! That was amazing!! I've always wanted to fly!! And it also works just like the ring; I only need to think about flying, and it would do its job. And the last thing I got were cool-looking sunglasses. I also put them on. It felt like I was in the Batman movie of when he wears his mask; it tells him where danger lays, and he can see things in X-ray vision. Awesome!

I was so thankful for all this effort they put in for making these for me. I thanked them all for their challenging work for me, and happily tested them out, outside. I took Atles with me to help me get used to how they work. I have always wanted to have superpowers, and now thanks to my new gadgets, it's like I really do.

They let me stay on their planet as long as I pleased. Even though I would love to stay here longer on this beautiful planet full of nice Komitaz, I couldn't stay. I have been gone for too long now. My parents would start worrying. So, I put my gadgets in my suitcase and told Atles to take me back home. He started his ship, but before we were about to leave, Aton came rushing into the ship. He came to me and said, "I hope you come back to visit me from time to time, my heroine." He then gave me a beautifully shaped Ikvi crystal and said "Take this with you, so that you would never forget this planet ... or forget me." I smiled and took it with a lot of gratitude. Then he said his goodbyes, and we finally took off. I noticed Atles was looking angry for some reason. I said, "What's the matter?" He ignored me. I decided to ignore him too, I can play that game too, stupid alien. I then looked at space and the beautiful stars and planets. Less than three hours later, and we were already there. Komitaz spaceships are much faster than human spaceships. I bet if humans would use their spaceship to go to Planet Komitaz, it would take them more than a thousand years to finally arrive there.

Atles landed his ship in the woods in front of my house. I got off the ship and looked at Atles and said, "So, I guess this is goodbye, right" He looked at me with his usual poker face and said, "Yes, it is." Even though he was right in front of me, I already missed him. Then I quickly said, "You can always come back to visit me, OK?" He agreed and smiled at me. Before he went back inside the ship to leave, I ran to him and hugged him from behind and said, "You'd better come back. Remember, you're not getting rid of me that easily, alien." He laughed the cutest laugh I have ever heard, and then he said, "The bracelet device you were given, we can use it to call each other anytime we want, so this isn't a real farewell. We can still have contact with each other" I looked at my bracelet device and smiled. Then before he left, he said, "If you need help or if anything happens, you can call me anytime. I will come to you as fast as I can." I thanked him for being such a nice friend. He smiled at me and went inside the ship, started it, and left with high speed. He was out of sight within seconds.

Wow, I seriously can't believe that this all really happened. I went into space, went to a different planet, met a new race, raided Area 51 and got shot by a gun. This was all one heck of an adventure. I bet if I told anyone what I did they would never even believe me.

The sun just came up. I quickly went back home; I missed my parents so much. I knocked on the door, and Danny opened it. He welcomed me in with a smile. And then my mother came to me and said, "Did you have fun with your friend?" I smiled and said, "Yup, it was the best experience I've had in a long time." She smiled at me. They all warmly welcomed me, and my mother even made my favorite food: lasagna!! Yummy! Finally, some tasty food. I almost starved myself on that planet. After that, we watched a movie, ate popcorn together and went to visit some family. There, I hung out with my best, cousin Farah. She and I grew up together; were just like sisters. Just like me, she has interests in anime and likes to draw. When we were little, we used to go to school together, too. Those were the best years for us; we did whatever we wanted back then, and nothing stopped us from having fun. We didn't care about anything and talked about imaginary things and magical places, like castles in the clouds. We were happy. Too bad our grades weren't the best back then. We almost never studied and kept getting bad grades. Anyway, if Farah found out that I have an alien friend, she would love to meet him. As I said, we both love the same things. When we were little, we used to wear the same clothes, like we were twins or something. We talked about anime the whole time I was there, and when it was getting late, we went back home, and I went to bed right away. Finally! Some rest.

CHAPTER 3

Bad or Good News?

The next couple of weeks went by simply fine. I went shopping with my mother, even though I hate shopping. You might think that a girl like me would die just to go shopping but, not me. I despise shopping, it's just so boring. I am more of a person who only wears clothes so I wouldn't be naked. I simply don't care about it. As long as I have something to wear, it's fine by me. So, if you ask me, I prefer to be at home drawing and watching anime, like the nerdy *weeb* I am. I also went swimming with Farah. She still doesn't have a swimming diploma, so I was teaching her how to swim.

I had a lot of fun these past peaceful weeks but, I kept getting the feeling that this is not the real me. When I was back on Planet Komitaz training and even when I was raiding Area 51, I felt like I found the real me – the girl who loves adventures and manages to save the day. I really missed those times, even the dangerous moments where I almost got killed. But now that I think about it, It's strange that, even though I raided Area 51 and killed so many soldiers, it still hasn't even become some sort of news. I was really expecting a huge breaking news story and that the entire world would be talking about the mysterious girl who raided Area 51 and beat all the military soldiers there. But there is nothing on the news. Weird. Oh well. Maybe they're too ashamed to admit that one little girl was able to do all that. That is when I realized that I actually killed people. I felt guilty but, I also didn't have much of a choice. The whole Earth was in danger.

Something bad happened on the news channel. There was the evil scientist talking about the raid in Area 51. It was the scientist, the one who was supposed to be dead after I shot him. He was bleeding out and I set off a nuclear bomb. How is he still alive? I guess he has nine lives or something. He talked about what happened at Area 51 and that it was a girl who did it single handedly. Even though this was bad, I somehow liked how much attention I got. The major news story was about me. It did not take long until the entire world was talking about the mysterious girl who raided Area 51.

I quickly grabbed my bracelet device that was given to me by the Komitaz. I wanted to contact Atles to tell him about the evil scientist and the breaking news. I pushed the button, and the bracelet device spoke and said, "Who would you like to call? State their name." Cool! They even put it in my language. Those Komitaz are just so smart. I then said, "I would like to talk to Atles." The button turned green, and then I heard Atles's voice coming out of it. He said, "Hello, Tayler?" I was so happy to hear his voice. I felt my heart beating faster from the excitement. I quickly replied, "Wow, it's been a while, hasn't it, Atles? Why didn't you call me or anything, after all this time?" He then said, "Sorry, I was very busy lately, and I thought maybe you would be pretty busy, too, with your schoolwork and family business." I laughed and said, "Nice excuse for ignoring me all this time." Oh well. It's OK. I called because something, I think, bad or good happened. I'm not sure how to feel about it." He then said, "Tell me what happened." I then explained to him that the evil scientist, whose name is Dr. Brandon, by the way, survived the raid and told everyone about what happened and that the whole Earth is talking about that incident. He reassured me and said, "Don't worry. As long as nobody knows it was you, everything will be fine. And, then after some time, people will start to forget about it ... hopefully." I nodded and then talked about the past few days and about how bored I got since he left. We chatted for hours, mostly I did the talking, while Atles listened to me patiently. When there was nothing more to talk about, we said our goodbyes and ended the call. It was nice talking to him, but it didn't feel the same since he wasn't really here with me. I know he has his own life and plans, so I didn't tell him to come here. It's fine, I guess. But why does my heart feel so weird?

CHAPTER 4

More Weirdness?!

A couple of peaceful and normal months passed by. It was midnight when I went outside, walking through the woods. I then went to the spot where I met Atles for the first time. This is my happy place. I come here to think about my secret adventure. Any other person would be scared walking in the dark woods in the middle of the night like this, but not me, not after everything I went through. It's actually strange. Before I met Atles, I used to be a shy and cowardly girl, who had trouble sleeping sometimes because I was scared and anxious all the time. But now I'm not scared anymore. It's like those feelings all disappeared inside of me. I feel way more confident now. I also don't have stress stomach cramps anymore. That's all thanks to Atles.

While I was daydreaming, I heard footsteps. I then stopped and heard them getting closer to me. I stood still while I was trying to figure out what to do, but before I could do anything, a broad man with feathery wings, a strange chestnut brown outfit and clear white skin with white eyes was before me. I looked at him, shocked, knowing that he was certainly no human. What the hell is it with these strange creatures always appearing in these woods!? The way he looked at me was different than the way Atles looked at me the first time. This is a thousand times scarier. It's like he wanted to do something bad to me. Well, I didn't want to know what he wanted from me, So I slowly put my hand in my pocket to take out the invisibility ring, but then he spoke in a low scary voice. "I wouldn't do that if I were you."

I froze and said, "Who are you, and what do you want?" He came awfully close to me, ignoring my personal space. He was so big and tall. I looked so small in front of him. Before I could do anything, he raised his big hands with sharp nails to my face. A light came out of his hand. Then suddenly, I felt dizzy, and everything went black ...

Gladiators

I opened my eyes and heard a large crowd cheering. When I looked at the people around me, I realized that they weren't human or Komitaz. They were some sort of scary monsters with black wings, sharp claws, and fangs. I was in some sort of arena. I looked around and saw a couple of human bones lying around the place. I also saw spatters of blood all around the arena. My heart started anxiously beating faster. I felt a little sick to the stomach, seeing all the human bones in front of me.

Then suddenly everyone started a countdown. when they finished counting, a large door opened, and a bunch of scary-looking monsters came running at me with their dangerous claws and spears. I started running away from them barely dodging their attacks. Why do these kinds of stuff keep happening to me?? When I said I wanted another adventure, I didn't mean this.

Then I saw a human boy, who was hiding behind a large boulder. He was sent here just like me. I saw a monster ready to grab him from behind, so, without thinking, I flew with my flying Komitaz shoe soles and pushed the boy out of the way. I then punched the monster and quickly grabbed the boy's hand and ran to a safer spot. Then, when I looked around the place, I saw a portal. When I looked at the portal, I saw that it would lead us back home from where we were kidnapped. Actually, there were two portals: one would lead back to the woods, where I was kidnapped and one would lead to a little playground, which must be where the little boy was kidnapped from. Whatever this was, I think this thing is about surviving the monsters and running back home through those portals. This was apparently some type of game where your life is at stake. It reminds me of the movie *Gladiator*, where the gladiators are supposed to fight for the people's and the king's entertainment.

I looked at the little boy, who was petrified by all this. Lucky for him, he was with someone who isn't new to weird things happening. I then saw a couple of monsters coming toward us, so I turned to the boy and said, "You see that portal over there? I'm going to distract the monsters, and you make sure to run inside the portal as fast as possible. Don't look back. Just run, OK?" He nodded his head. I then ran the other way and flew around the place to keep the attention to me. It worked, they all set their attention on me and came after me. Before I started to run away, I looked back and saw that the boy made it in the portal safely. Good. Now I only need to worry about getting myself to safety. So, I landed and ran toward the portal, but suddenly the ground cracked open, making a hole. I could make it if I flew, but the moment, I wanted to fly, I got pulled back by a female monster that had long black hair, sharp teeth, and long sharp claws. I tried to get out of her grasp, but we both ended falling inside the hole in the ground. I grabbed the sides and quickly climbed up. I was about to go through the portal, but I stopped and looked back at the female monster. She was holding the sides nearly falling down the hole, where there was no end to see. Her scared face reminded me of the poor Komitaz who were captured in Area 51. So, before I could think it through, I held my hand out and shouted, "Here! Quickly! Hold my hand!" The female monster looked at me confused, and, after some consideration, she grabbed my hand. Man, she sure was heavy. I then used all my strength and pulled her to safety. I can't believe I just saved some monster who was trying to kill me. I'm an idiot. Then, I noticed that the crowd went silent. I looked around and saw that they were all looking at me, confused, so before anything else happened, I quickly went inside the portal.

I then finally came back to the woods I got snatched from. I ran back home, quietly went to the bathroom, and took a long, warm bath before my family would see my dirty torn clothes and muddy face. I looked at my arm and saw that my skin was badly scratched. It must have happened when the female monster grabbed me with her sharp claws. I felt a burning pain. I then bandaged it tightly so that it wouldn't bleed anymore. Why did I even save that being who tried to kill me?

For the next two weeks, I was trying to contact Atles to tell him what happened to me. But he wouldn't contact me back. I'm starting to get worried about him. I hope nothing happened to him in space, and I hope I don't encounter those weird monsters again. This does explain why there has been a lot of people who have gone missing these past months. All those people that were missing were just kidnapped by those monsters. Judging by all the bones and blood I saw back at the arena, I'm not sure they are alive anymore. I don't even want to know how those horrible monsters killed them. They are cruel barbaric monsters.

The next month went by very normally. Unfortunately, I still didn't get in contact with Atles, but thankfully I didn't encounter any monsters either. Why do these weird things keep happening to me so suddenly? First, I was a normal girl with a normal life, and now I just can't seem to get back to my normal life. I can't believe that the day would come that I would hope to have a normal boring life. I guess an adventure is not always a fun experience. The bones that I saw in the arena are still stuck in my head. All those innocent people slaughtered only for entertainment.

Then, I gave up on trying to contact Atles and started focusing on my own normal life without aliens or monsters. I contacted my best friend Anne and made some plans with her to go to the movies. There is a new movie out that seems interesting. Of course, she was more than happy to meet up. We were to meet up on Saturday. This is the perfect opportunity to just focus on myself and my own life and not think of him anymore. I really needed some distraction from all the action.

Saturday

I cycled to the cinema where I saw Anne waiting outside, busy on her phone. She smiled when she looked up and saw me. She said, "Hey, it sure has been a while hasn't it? When was the last time we did anything fun together?" I replied, "Sorry, things were a bit complicated ... and I was terribly busy with ... other stuff." She analyzed me and said, "Have you fallen in love?" I looked at her with wide open eyes and quickly said "I ... No, I am not interested in anyone!! Why would you say that?" She laughed and said, "I can see it in your eyes. You seem to be missing someone you really like, and I am your best friend ... I know that kind of stuff." I quickly said, "Well, you are wrong. I don't like anyone, and I most certainly do not miss anyone!" I said that with a lot of certainty, but then I started wondering who I wanted to convince, Anne or myself ...

We then went inside, bought some popcorn, some drinks and went to our seats. The movie was about aliens abducting people, and there was a new superhero, who would kill the alien and save the people from the alien spaceships. Why am I not surprised? Just when I wanted to think about something else.

I couldn't concentrate on the movie. Atles kept coming to mind, and as much as I don't want to admit it, I missed him and was very worried about him.

The movie is three hours long. In the middle of the movie, I left to go to the restroom. I was washing my hands, when suddenly a voice called my name. I looked around in surprise, but there was no one there. I felt uncomfortable and had a feeling that I was being watched by something or someone. So, I quickly ran back to Anne and back to my seat. I hoped that my mind was just playing games with me, because I was not in any mood to be kidnapped again or to associate with a weird being again. When the movie was finally over, it was dark outside. I said my goodbyes to Anne, who got picked up by her mom. I got on my bike and headed home. The road was dark and empty ... not a soul to be seen. I heard owls howling. If I didn't have my invisible ring and my flying shoe soles to protect myself with, I would be really scared right now. That's when I heard the voice again.

"Tayler ..."

I stopped, got off my bike and looked around. There was no one to be seen. I quickly got out my invisible ring and became invisible. There was no way those weird beings were going to kidnap me twice; I'm not called the "Great Komitaz Heroine" for nothing or whatever they are calling me here on Earth – the Area 51 Raider.

"That pathetic Komitaz ring cannot hide you from my eyes."

I gasped. That is impossible. I let myself be visible again and shouted, "Where are you, and what do you want!? Show yourself! I'm not afraid of you!" It's true. I wasn't afraid; I was terrified. Now that my ring was of no use to me, I felt a little helpless. Too bad the Komitaz didn't give me the bracelet gun I used to raid Area 51. But even though I wanted to keep the Komitaz gun, the leader of the Komitaz told me that it was not wise to let such a powerful weapon be on Earth. So, he took that from me and gave me an invisible ring, X-ray glasses and flying shoe soles instead.

I have nothing to protect myself with or be able to fight with. So, in other words, I can only run or hide. It was quiet, I thought the thing left, but just when I wanted to walk back to my bike and get out of here, I heard footsteps. I turned around to look where I heard it and saw a black silhouette not too far from me. I couldn't see his face, so I went a little closer, and he opened these wings wide open. He came into the light of the street lanterns, and I scanned him. He was tall, had long black hair, scary crimson eyes, pale skin, a scar on his face, and black feathery wings. He was of sturdy build. There was no way I could take him out. If I tried anything, he could easily throw me to the other side of the Earth.

He then spoke and said in a husky voice, "I know who you are, Tayler Star." I just stood there shocked by how he knew my full name. He then continued and said, "I have done some research about you, and I know that you saved Earth from those Komitaz freaks." I wouldn't just stand here and let him offend the Komitaz race anymore, so I said, "They aren't freaks –

He interrupted me and said, "Oh, so you like them that much that you're willing to defend them even in this situation, where you can't even defend yourself? You're not as smart as I thought."

I ignored his remark and said, "Just tell me what you want from me." He looked at me.

He was surprised that I was still brave enough to stand there and talk to him despite the dangerous situation I was in. "Tell me, heroine, are you really that tough or just stupid enough to put yourself in danger without having a weapon or a way to protect yourself?"

I didn't know what to say. He was right, though. I was stupid enough to test him and stand up for the Komitaz race, even though this demon or monster could kill me in a second if he wanted to. I'm risking my life for no reason.

Then a thought came to me: If he really wanted to kill me, he could have done it by now. This unexpected thought made me feel less scared now. So, I straightened my back, looked him right in the eyes and told him, "Just tell me what you want from me. I'm not scared of you or of death."

He looked at me, surprised. It seemed like he believed that I wasn't scared and that I was brave, which wasn't really the case. I was terrified of him and of death, but he didn't need to know that.

Stranger Perspective

Ever since I saw her using these gadgets and helping one of my kind, I have been following this strange girl for some time. I found out that she worked with the Komitaz and that it was her from the news. The girl who raided Area 51. I wasn't very shocked by her bravery. You needed guts to do the things she did.

So, I then said, "We are the Kultraz. We are a race that lived years before you humans came." She looked at me, interested in what I had to say. So, I continued. "We met the Komitaz before you humans were ever on Earth. ... Back then, we, the Kultraz, were the only living beings alive on planet Earth. After that, the dinosaurs appeared, then the animals, and then, at last, you humans appeared. When you humans appeared, you took our lands on Earth and made up stories about the Kultraz. You called us demons and monsters. ... Because of your race, we had to go into hiding, away from humans' eyes."

The human girl looked at me with a concerned and pity look. I could not believe it; she really was different. At last, I told her the very thing I wanted to know about her. "But, despite your situation back in that arena, you did not only save the human boy, but you also saved the female Kultraz, who even tried to kill you from the start. I want to know why you did that."

Back to Tayler POV

I felt sorry for their kind. I can't believe that humans were discriminating and making enemies out of other races. First, it was with the Komitaz that could have led to a war that we humans would have never won, and now I find out that the humans also discriminated against an ancient race that was here before us. They have lived on Earth for so long and still got robed from their lands. It's like the guests have taken over the owners house. Sometimes I hate being a part of the human race. This is just wrong.

The Kultraz then said in a louder and irritated voice, "Well, what was your reason?!" I was so lost in my thought I forgot to answer him. He sure has a hot temper.

So, I said, "Well, I'm not so sure. I just thought she looked like the helpless Komitaz back at Area 51, so I just saved her without even thinking about it." He looked like he was trying to figure out what I just said, then he looked at me with his crimson eyes. Then, before he could say anything, there were some drunk guys walking down the street behind me. I looked behind me, and, when I looked back in front of me, he was gone. He just disappeared. I then got on my bike and hurriedly cycled home without looking back even once.

I sigh in relief. I thought I was never going to get home.

CHAPTER 5

Back To Normal

For the next couple of days, I stayed home. I was not going to risk another encounter with the Kultraz race. I am done with weird things happening to me. Now, I just want to go back to living my own normal boring and very safe life. I thought I missed my heroic self but, I was wrong. I am not a hero, I am not strong. I am just a weak little girl that still can't protect herself. Whatever happened in Area 51 was just dumb luck. I should stop pretending to be something I am not...

About a month passed by, and I didn't even try to call Atles after my encounter with the scary Kultraz. I'm done with Atles and everything else that keeps happening. I have to keep focusing on my own life now. My birthday was coming up, I'm finally turning eighteen. I'm going to be old enough to live by myself, and I can also legally adopt someone. Anne jokingly told me to adopt her, since she wants to live with me. She is still seventeen, five months younger than me. Sometimes Anne and I would talk about moving into a house together and becoming roommates, just like in the movies. I told her that she could come live with me after she turned eighteen. She was so excited she was already packing her stuff. That Anne – she never fails to make me laugh.

My parents aren't kicking me out or anything; in fact, they wish I would stay. But if I don't want anything happening to them, I had to move away from them and live someplace else. I cannot risk putting their lives in danger.

I decided to take a part-time job, so that I could pay the rent. I chose to apply for a job nearby my new apartment. I

applied for a job in a small store that sold all kinds of crystals and rocks. Thankfully, the owner was nice. She was an old lady named Sara. She started this business when she was my age. She was more than happy to let me work with her and help her out in the store. It was a cute little store, where two or three customers would appear every day. It was the perfect job to help me relax and let my mind relax.

After the job interview, I went back home and started making some sketches. I haven't been able to draw in a long while.

I then thought about the Kultraz I encountered that night. He was scary, but I had to say he wasn't that bad looking. I tried to make a sketch of him in my own style.

I remember all too well what he looked like. His wings were so beautiful they were like an angel's wings, but in black. And, he had this huge scar on his face. I wonder how he got it. I made the sketch but didn't post it.

My Birthday

I was packing my stuff and taking them all to my apartment with my father's help. I felt a little scared to leave so suddenly. I have always been with my family, and now I was moving away to stay in an apartment all by myself. I should adopt a pet to keep me company, but come to think of it, I'm afraid of touching animals.

The reason I'm so scared of touching animals is because when I was little, I was bitten by a dog. My parents quickly took me to the doctor to see if I got any infections or maybe rabies. Thankfully, I didn't have any of those. Another time, I was chased by a stray dog that lived somewhere in my neighborhood. He also wanted to bite me for some reason. I quickly went back inside before he could bite me. That day I thought I escaped death. It was the most terrifying encounter I ever had with a dog.

So, yea, I really have a bad history with dogs. As for cats, I'm a little allergic to them, and I'm afraid they would scratch me. I have seen online videos of how a bunch of cat owners must deal with their scary, aggressive cats, who would suddenly attack their owners for no reason. I don't think I want an aggressive unpredictable cat.

I guess I could buy a goldfish. I don't need to touch it or take it for a walk. All I need to do is give it food every day. How hard can that be? I hope I don't forget to feed it, though.

I came back home with my dad to pick up my last box of stuff. When I opened the front door – "SURPRISE!!"

I fell over the floor. Everyone laughed at my reaction. My whole family and Anne were here. I didn't know when they had planned all this. I had even forgotten that it was my birthday with all the moving I was doing. The whole house was decorated, and there was a huge chocolate cake with my name on it. I couldn't believe it; I really love my family and Anne, too, of course. I strictly told everyone not to sing "Happy Birthday" to me, because it was so cringey. Instead, they played some pop songs. I blew out the candles, and I thanked everyone for the gifts. Most of them got me money, which was the perfect gift since I could buy things I actually like with the money. Anne got me a beautiful, limited edition Zorro action figure from One Piece. I always wanted to buy it, but it was so expensive. I felt the excitement filling me; I tightly hugged her and told her how amazing she is for buying this expensive thing for me. She laughed at my reaction and said that I was worth it. I just couldn't stop smiling even though my cheeks started to hurt. Everyone else said that I was too old to be getting dolls. I didn't listen to them; you are never old for anime.

He Is Here

I was finishing cleaning the store and putting new rocks on the shelves. I had moved into my apartment and have been living alone for a week now. It was scary at first, but I'm used to it now. I even bought a goldfish; I really needed the company. It was getting late. I said my goodbyes to Sara and headed back home. Just when I was about to get inside the building, a familiar voice said "Hey, long time, no see." I turned around, and it was him. I can't believe my eyes. He was really there. I ran up to him, hugged him tightly and closed my eyes. Atles chuckled, put his arms around me and said, "Sorry that I didn't respond to your calls. My communicator broke and, when I fixed it, I saw all the missed calls from you, so I came here as fast as a could." I felt so safe in his arms. Since I encountered the Kultraz, I have been feeling anxious nowadays. Everywhere I went, I kept looking behind me, afraid that the Kultraz would appear out of nowhere again. I parted from him and looked at him. He gently smiled at me. I then said, "There is a lot of stuff I need to tell you." He just nodded, and I let him in my apartment. I told him to make himself at home. He sat on the couch and waited patiently for me. I made some tea and got out the cookies I bought earlier. I set it all on the table next to the couch and sat next to him.

"OK, before I start, I need to know if you are familiar with the Kultraz race." He looked at me with wide eyes and said, "How do you know of their existence?"

I responded, "Just, first tell me what you know about them."

He sat up straight, looked at me with his usual poker face and said, "All I know is that the Kultraz were the first living beings that appeared on Earth. When we discovered the new life, we went to Earth to meet them, but we soon found out that they are a cocky and powerful race who didn't want to associate with other races. The Kultraz have the power to change the course of events with supernatural powers that they acquired with the Wikva." I asked what that was. He continued, "The Wikva is a giant colorful, precious stone that they have on their island just here on Earth. It lays on the middle of the island. It is also where their kingdom is. We weren't able to create a bond with them because they were worried that we would steal their precious stone. That is all I know about them." I just sat there trying to process everything he just told me. I couldn't believe it. There is a secret island filled with ancient beings who were here since the beginning of time. But how is it that humans never found this island? I asked Atles, and he told me that they use some sort of magic to hide their very existence from us humans. Now I understood what the Kultraz meant when he said that they hid from the human eye. They made themselves and their island invisible from us. This keeps getting more interesting. I never thought Earth would turn from a boring world to a more interesting and magical place. To think that magic actually exists.

Atles then asked, "How do you know about them?" I then told him everything that happened to me these past few months. He looked at the ground, and I saw how his face turn from a poker face to an angry face. When I finished telling him everything, he looked at me, and his face softened. He then held my hand, making my heart skip a beat. He then said in a soft gentle voice, "I'm sorry for not have been here with you to protect you from these dangerous beings. If only my communicator didn't break, I could've come here sooner and stayed here to protect you from them." I smiled and said, "It's OK. You don't need to beat yourself up with it ... besides, I raided Area 51, remember? I can protect myself just fine." He closed his eyes and squeezed my hand a little. I felt relieved, I was so glad he was here. I actually lied, I wasn't really capable of protecting myself, and every time I encountered those Kultraz, I had a big chance of getting killed. I felt my eyelids getting heavier. I just came from work. I was so excited to see Atles again that I forgot I was tired. So, I put my head on his shoulders and fell asleep with a smile on my face. The last thing I felt was a soft hand caressing my cheeks ...

Atles Perspective

I need to fix this communicator in case Tayler calls me; I have been so busy working I forgot that I still have to fix it. During these past couple of months, I have been traveling around space looking for things that haven't been found or discovered.

Ever since we built ships that could travel at the speed of light, we have been exploring the universe looking for other life forms or planets with interesting raw materials. Our planet may not have a lot of raw material to use to survive on the planet, but thanks to our intelligence, we were able to make everything we need to survive, with only the Ikvi. The Ikvi is a beautiful and extremely useful purple material that can be used to make our clothes, houses and weapons. The material is also edible, so we make our food with it. It may not taste good, but it is extremely healthy and helps us grow in a healthy condition. I went back home to Komitaz and decided to finally fix my communicator device. On my way to the lab where we make our gadgets, I met Maver. He greeted me and said, "How is Tayler doing? Do you still have contact with her?" I told him that I was trying to have contact with her by fixing my communicator device. He nodded and said, "Well, I guess that explains your behavior the last couple of days." I looked at him with confusion and said, "What do you mean?" He then said that I was acting a little more aggressive these days and the reason was because I missed Tayler. I quickly responded to him and said, "I don't miss her! She is just a human friend that miraculously forced me to befriend her. How can I, a Komitaz, ever even have feelings for her, a human ... don't spread these equivocate rumors." That came

73

out a bit more aggressive than I wanted to. I then thought about who I was trying to persuade.

Maver didn't say anything. He smirked and walked away to go on another search mission. I headed straight to the lab. Even if I did have feelings, why would a human ever fall in love with another race that looks so different than them? I bet she saw me only as a weird alien friend. I tried to ignore these thoughts and focus on fixing this device. It didn't take long. I realized it wasn't fully broken; it just needed some new parts to make it work again. After I fixed it, I looked at my missed calls. I saw that Tayler called me a couple of times. Something must have happened. I tried to call her, but she wouldn't answer. I needed to head back to Earth to see what she needed from me.

I landed in the woods in front of her house, where I first met her. I made myself invisible, thanks to my ring, and went to her house. I used the flying shoes to fly up to her window, but I saw that her room was empty. Even her precious figures weren't there anymore. I used my communicator to look for the signal of her bracelet device. I saw that she is someplace far away from this town. She did once tell me that she was almost old enough to move out of her house, so I guess she must have moved someplace else to live. I flew to the location, camouflaged my ship, and it didn't take long before I spotted her. She was walking alone. I quietly walked up to her and said, "Hey, long time no see." She turned around, and I felt a lightness in my chest. She ran up to me and hugged me tightly. I hugged her back. Usually, we Komitaz don't show our emotions with physical contact, but I learned that humans do, so I just cope with it and try my best to properly communicate with her.

I then said, "Sorry that I didn't respond to your calls. My communicator broke and, when I fixed it, I saw all the missed calls from you, so I came here as fast as a could." She smiled at me, and I smiled back. She then said, "There is a lot of stuff I need to tell you." I really missed her cute voice. I then followed her inside the building. I sat on the couch and waited for her. Of course, knowing her, she would get me something delicious again. She put the food and drinks on the table. I didn't know what it was, but judging from the delicious aroma it had, It was going to taste good, for sure. She then sat next to me and looked at me with her beautiful big brown eyes and said, "OK. Before I start, I need to know if you are familiar with the Kultraz." My eyes widened. How does she know about them? I thought the Kultraz were supposed to hide themselves from the humans. I then said, "How do you know of their existence?" She then responded and said, "Just, first tell me what you now about them." I told her everything I knew about them, and she was interested in what I told her. I then asked again, "How do you know about them?" She then told me everything that happened to her ever since I left her. I looked at the ground and felt my anger rising from within me. I felt so pathetic for not being here to protect her from those brutal beings.

When she finished, she looked at me and, just by looking at her, I felt more relaxed. I held her hand and apologized to her for not being here to protect her. She gave me a beautiful smile and said," It's OK. You don't need to beat yourself up with it. Besides, I raided Area 51, remember? I can protect myself just fine." I closed my eyes and knew she was lying; I just know that she was scared. I squeezed her hand a little. She let out a sigh, and she rested her head on my shoulder. I caressed her cheek and promised that I would fix this. I would make sure these Kultraz would leave her alone. I then carried her to her room, put her on her bed and went back to the living room to have a taste of the strange liquid she brought to me and the hard brown round things. I tasted them and, just as I thought, they were delicious.

The Unexpected Savior

Tayler's POV

I woke up on my bed. Went to the living room, and he wasn't here anymore. My heart sunk. Don't tell me he left again; he just got here. I looked at the clock and realized I needed to go to work. So, I put some decent clothes on, ate breakfast and left the apartment. I worked till late. It sure was crowded today. Usually, the store gets only two or three costumers per day, but today, the whole store was full. So, I had to work extra hard and got extra tired. Apparently crystals were a trend now. A lot of popular people on social media showed off their collection on-line. So, it didn't take long before it became a trend, and a lot of people wanted to buy as many as they could. When it was closing time, I threw out the garbage and said my goodbyes to Sara and walked back to my apartment. When I was home, he wasn't there. *sigh* I got a little frustrated. I then fed my little goldfish and went outside to look for him.

I walked around outside; I felt the chilly wind on my skin and heard the owls howling through the night. I looked at the beautiful starry sky and breathed in the fresh chilly air. There was no one around. Everyone was sleeping or working late-night shifts. I wandered around the area and started missing Chesterville for some reason. I missed the old play-grounds I used to go to when I was a kid, and I missed the familiar streets and the houses I would walk by every day. I was so lost in my mind I didn't hear anything around me. I was completely lost in my thoughts and felt a little irritated that Atles was nowhere to be seen.

Then, suddenly, I felt someone forcefully grab me and put his hand on my mouth, so that I wouldn't scream. I tried to get out of his grasp, but he was too strong. I literally saw my life flash before my eyes. I tightly closed my eyes and knew that I was done for. This was really it ...

Then, I heard the kidnapper groan in pain. Someone hit the man from behind. After he got hit again, he let me go. I fell to the ground. My whole body was trembling, I couldn't even stand. The man then screamed like he saw a ghost or something and ran away. Was it him? The figure came closer to me and helped me up, I looked at him and couldn't believe who it was.

The person that saved me was the female Kultraz, who I saved back when I was kidnapped by the Kultraz. I just looked at her shocked to see her again. She looked at me with her clear white eyes. I then said, "Thank you … you really saved my life. God knows what he wanted to do to me." The female Kultraz didn't say anything, so I said, "My name is Tayler Star. What can I call you?" She then pointed at herself as if she had trouble speaking and said,

"Me … Ikaza."

After she saved me and told me her name, I felt less scared of her. I analyzed her. She wore a gray torn-up dress, her long black hair was almost all over her face, she had white skin with scratches here and there on her body. What got my attention was that she didn't have wings. Maybe not all Kultraz have wings, I guess. I decided not to ask about that in case I offend her.

I welcomed her to come to my apartment, but just when she was coming closer to me, someone shouted, "Stay right there!" It was Atles. So, he didn't leave to Planet Komitaz after all. He pushed me behind him, trying to protect me from her. Ikaza backed away, scared that Atles would hurt her. I then quickly came in between them and explained to Atles that she saved me from someone who tried to kidnap me. He then relaxed and stared at Ikaza. Just when I wanted to invite her in again, a portal behind her opened, and she jumped right in. The portal then disappeared.

I guess Atles really scared her off. I looked at Atles and said, "Look what you did, you idiot! I was about to make friends with her ... and where did you run off to anyway? You know you can't just leave without saying anything!" He looked at me, offended, which he should be. He always makes me worry about him without realizing it, stupid alien. *sigh* I then went back home. I needed to think. Who was it that wanted to kidnap me? Was it just a random kidnapper or someone who had his eyes on me? Whatever it was, I was not safe to be alone anymore. I was lucky Ikaza showed up, otherwise I wouldn't be here now. Atles followed me back to my apartment and stayed close to me. I kept ignoring him. This went on for a couple of minutes. Then, he finally snapped and said, "OK, I'm sorry. I was wrong to leave without saying anything, and I was wrong to judge the situation without knowing what happened." I calmed down and forgave him. He then tried to hold my hand, but I slapped it away, went to my room and closed the door behind me. I then heard him say, "Hey, I thought you forgave me?" I ignored him and went to bed. I guess even male Komitaz have a hard time understanding women's feelings. I wouldn't really break it to him. Even I don't understand myself sometimes.

Anyway, I needed to rest after what I had to endure. One thing I'm certain of: My life is not going to go back the way it was, so I just had to embrace the weirdness and just live my life as normally as I could.

CHAPTER 6

Double Trouble

One week later, summer vacation ended, and I already had chosen to have a gap year so that I could have time to decide what I wanted to do for a career. I still haven't decided it. I always wanted to become a professional artist but, seeing how underappreciated we artists are in this society, I must choose something that could provide me a strong and safe future. So, I have an entire year to think about it. It's supposed to give me enough time, but, of course, I always stress about making big decisions that could change the course of my future.

Atles was still with me, acting like my personal bodyguard. Wherever I went, he would follow me and use his invisible ring to stay with me without causing unnecessary attention. I have to say it is sweet of him to stay here on a foreign planet only to protect me. He really is a good friend. I am also happy with the company. After all living by yourself can really feel lonely sometimes.

It was late, and I was buying ice cream for the both of us. I got chocolate-flavored ice cream, of course, and Atles got the chocolate, too. We went to a little playground that was near my apartment. Since it was late, no one was outside, so Atles became visible again. We sat on the swings, which would squeak every time we moved a little on them. We finished our ice cream, and I could see that Atles enjoyed it. Of course, he enjoyed it its chocolate ice cream after all. I bet if I got him strawberry-flavored ice cream, he wouldn't be able to finish it.

It was quiet. We didn't say anything; we just enjoyed the relaxing peaceful night. It was raining earlier, so the smell of rain was all around us. I breathed it in. The rainy smell filled my nose. The wind kept blowing my hair on my face, so I put my hair in a ponytail. It was getting late so, I stood up and headed back. Atles followed my lead.

But then we heard a loud thud behind us. We quickly turned around. It was the Kultraz that followed me the other time, his crimson eyes were piercing right through Atles's pitch-black eyes. He then said, with a husky voice, "SO! Komitaz freak, you think you can threaten our kind and get away with it?!" Oh no. Ikaza must have told him how Atles threatened her. This was all a misunderstanding. I needed to fix this before it got out of hand. So, I stood in front of Atles, trying to stop him from walking closer to the Kultraz. If there is one thing, I know: It's that both of them are hotheads, and it is unwise to let two hotheads fight it out like barbarians.

So, I said, "I'm sorry. It was my fault. He was only trying to protect me. It was all a misunderstanding." He stared at me and said, "From what I heard, it was Ikaza who protected you, and yet she still got threatened." I then whispered to Atles to apologize to him. Atles refused and loudly said, "Why should I apologize to a race that kidnapped you and tried to kill you? From how I see it, he should be the one apologizing, and we should be the ones to be angry!" I had to admit he was right; they did kidnap me. If it wasn't for my Komitaz gadgets, I would be dead by now. I looked at the Kultraz, and he was smirking at us, like he didn't even care what his kind was doing to us humans. "You are going to pay for this, Komitaz. We Kultraz made it clear that your kind should not come to our planet Earth anymore. Wait till my father finds out that you not only stepped foot on our planet again but you also threatened our kind."

My whole body started to tremble. This was all my fault. Because of me, there will be a big conflict again. Just when the Kultraz opened his wings to fly away, I shouted, "WAIT!" He looked at me, and I said, "Please, this doesn't need to be bigger than it is. It was my fault; I asked him to come here, and I'm the one who told him to protect me from your kind. You should give me the fault, not him, please." He stood there staring at me without saying anything. He was thinking about it. He then said, "Well, I have to say, Tayler Star, you really like putting yourself in danger, don't you?" He smirked, and I just looked at him with a poker face. Atles looked at him as if he wanted to attack him any moment. I tried to calm him down by holding his arm back. He looked at me with his soft gaze and said, "You don't have to do this. Our rivalry began long before you humans appeared. This has nothing to do with you." I didn't listen to him because it really was my fault. If I wasn't stupid enough to go outside in the middle of the night, I wouldn't have been in danger, and Ikaza wouldn't have saved me, and Atles wouldn't have threatened her. This all happened because of my dumb decisions.

The Kultraz then continued and said, "If you want to take fault, then you must come with me and convince my race that it was you who opened the door for this outsider to come to our Earth." Despite my fear, I nodded. I had to be brave. Even though I'm scared, I would still do anything to keep peace on this planet and any other planet.

Atles tried to stop this by coming in between us, but the Kultraz punched him in the stomach so hard, making him fly a couple of yards away from me. When Atles fell on the ground, he was in a lot of pain, breathing heavily for air. I looked at him shocked and shouted at the Kultraz. "What do you think you're doing? This wasn't part of the deal, you idiot!!" He smirked at the sight and said, "I know, but I felt like doing that, and plus he shouldn't have come in between us." I couldn't believe it; he was worse than I thought. I tried to run to Atles, but the Kultraz grabbed me and carried me over his shoulders like a sack of potatoes. Before I could say anything, we were flying above in the sky. Then he opened a portal and flew right in it. Everything suddenly went dark …

The Hidden Island Of The Kultraz

I opened my eyes, and I had a bad, throbbing headache. Where was I? The last thing I remember was being carried and going inside a portal. I looked around to see where I was. I was in a large room with a lot of plants and trees in the room. How did they even plant trees in a house? The room was very colorful, and I could smell a pleasant aroma. I looked around and discovered that the aroma was coming from the beautiful flowers, which were growing everywhere in the room. I have never seen a flower like these before. It looked a little like a lily flower. The petals were big and red, and the stamen of the flower were dimly glowing. I gently touched the petals, but then the flower quickly closed. I quickly took my hand back in fear from the unexpected reaction of the flower.

I then saw a window; well if you call a hole in the wall a window. I went and looked outside. My eyes widened at the colorful beautiful scenery. I wasn't sure if this was really Earth. Was I dead? It felt like I was on another planet or something. There was no way this was still Earth. A little bird then appeared in my room; it must have been hiding under my bed. I looked at the bird, and I couldn't believe my eyes: It was a DODO! I thought the Dodos all died out a long time ago. How is this even possible?! He was so cute, but I didn't touch it. As cute as it may be, I'm still very afraid of animals. The door then opened, and the Kultraz who brought me here came in. He smirked at me. What is it with him and smirking? Well, I guess he did look handsome while doing it. Wait, what am I even saying? He's a jerk; I can't start liking him. He then spoke, "I see you met my little friend, Coco." I looked at his red eyes and said "Yes, but I thought dodos all died out?" He chuckled and said "We love Earth so much that we protect all kinds of animals from dying out. We have a lot more animals who were supposed to be dead ... like the mammoth, a couple of dinosaurs and a lot of wild plants and flowers that only grew a long time ago." I looked at him with a gaping mouth. Dinosaurs?! This is just the coolest thing ever. I always wanted to see what Dinos looked like in real life. I looked outside and saw the different kind of animals appear. I heard roars and other noises that I have never heard before. He was right; they were all still alive.

He then said, "I don't think I've introduced myself yet. I am Prince Merak, son of King Kurek." I looked at him, surprised, and said, "You are a real prince?" He chuckled and nodded. Wow! A real prince. Well, he wasn't like the nice gentle prince charming you would see in fantasy movies. I then said, "How did I pass out?" He answered, "Well, I guess you humans aren't strong enough to endure traveling through a long portal ... Going inside a portal that takes you somewhere too far away takes a lot of your energy, and if you are not so strong, you will pass out or ... even die." "WHAT?! I could have died!?" He laughed at my reaction and said, "I'm joking. You humans can't die. You just pass out. That's all. Besides, you went inside a portal once before, remember?" I then remembered that I did, indeed, go inside a portal when I was kidnapped by them, but I didn't pass out. I guess wherever that arena was, it was close to my home. But still, how dare he scare me like that? He doesn't act like a prince at all; he acts more like a child. So annoying.

He then told me to follow him to meet his father. I saw all the Kultraz looking at me while I was following Merak. I have to say associating with his kind so much made me less afraid of them. They didn't seem that bad. And, come to think of it, it wasn't my first time being in a place filled with other beings.

Merak then stopped and, in front of me was a throne with a grumpy-looking old Kultraz on it. I guess he was King Kurek. He looked at me, his red eyes piercing through my skin. My heart was beating like crazy; I was afraid of what he would say or do to me.

The king then spoke with a scary deep voice, "So, you must be the human that befriended the Komitaz and prevented them from starting a war against Earth." So they all knew who I was. I tried to be as confident and brave as possible, so I cleared my throat and said, "Yes!" Damn it, my voice cracked. Well, so much for wanting to be seen as a confident person. *sigh* Oh well. I looked next to me and saw Merak. He had his hand on his mouth, laughing as quietly as he could. I got irritated. So, I spoke again, "I mean, yes, that is me. And the reason I came here is to repay my thanks to the Kultraz named Ikaza, who saved me. I also wanted to apologize for my friend's behavior with her."

The king looked at me and laughed. He then said, "You don't need to worry, Tayler, the human. As long as I have been king, there has not been any conflict." I then remembered all the humans that were kidnapped and killed, and so I said, "What about the missing humans? You say that I don't need to worry, but how can I not be worried if I see my race getting kidnapped and killed?" He looked at me not knowing what I was talking about. Merak then interrupted and said, "I think this human has spoken enough." His father then raised his hand signaling his son to back down. The king then signaled for me to go on. I then continued. "I kept seeing on TV that there were people getting kidnapped. I didn't think it was that important, but then I was kidnapped myself, and if it wasn't for my Komitaz gadgets, I wouldn't be standing here right now."

The king got angry and looked at Merak and asked, "What is she talking about? I thought I was clear when I ordered the Kultraz to ignore the humans and stay out of their way?!" Merak got angry and shouted, "Why should we – the most powerful race of all – hide from a bunch of pathetic fragile beings that has taken every piece of land on Earth for themselves? We were here first!! We should be ruling over them and not hiding from them!!" The king then got up and slapped him across the face. I put my hands to my mouth shocked by this sudden act.

Merak turned around and flew out of the castle, through one of the windows in the room. The king then faced me again and said, "We are a race that respects everything the Earth creates, even you humans … A long time ago, when you humans appeared on Earth, we lived with you. But, after seeing that your race was afraid of us and just couldn't accept us, even though we were all born on this planet –" He coughed and then continued, "We decided to hide ourselves from you humans and came to this holy island of ours. What my son did is not right, I know that … but you should know that your race discriminated against us the second they met us. Not only that, but you humans also are slowly destroying our beloved Earth. I'm sure you are aware how the Earth's climate is changing. Those are the reason why my son has rebelled against me."

I just listened. He was right. We humans are destroying everything. I was surprised by how wise he is. What he said was a bit sad, though. We were all born on this planet and yet we just can't seem to get along. Planet Earth is also dying because of us humans, and no one is doing anything to help prevent it.

The king then said that the kidnappings won't happen anymore and that he would destroy the arena where the missing people were sent and killed. I was relieved that they would finally stop the killing. I then realized that this conflict is not something that could be fixed so easily. I needed to think of a way to fix this. I wonder what Atles is doing. I just hope he is not too worried about me. I must tell him that I need to fix this.

The king invited me for dinner. I accepted, of course. I was waiting in my room, then a female Kultraz, who introduced herself as Kabar, came to me. She had dark skin, wavy black hair, big yellow eyes, and beautiful brown wings. She was wearing a beautiful blue dress. She had brought me a colorful dress to wear at the dinner. The king had sent it. It was a traditional Kultraz dress for females. I usually don't wear dresses, but if I wanted them to like me, I would wear a dress, even though I hate wearing them. Kabar helped me put on the dress. I looked at my reflection in a large mirror that was hanging in the room. As much as I hated to admit it, I loved it; I felt like a beautiful princess. I twirled around happily.

Kabar then told me to follow her to the dinner table. I followed her into a large room. Everywhere, I looked there were trees and flowers growing inside the castle. They were so beautiful. I then saw the king sitting and waiting for me together with Merak. I quickly walked up to them and greeted them. The king complimented on how I looked in their traditional dresses, while Merak just stared at me. I sat next to the king, facing Merak on the other side. The king then started talking about how I raided Area 51, and every time I would answer, Merak would say one of his not-so-friendly remarks. So, once I got really angry at him, I kicked him under the table. His eyes widened at my sudden action. I then said, "Oops! My bad. Sometimes my body has a reflex of kicking people who deserve it." The king just looked at me surprised. Merak then smirked, meaning that he could also play that game. I was a bit scared that I had awakened a devil for myself. The king then said, "Why don't we just eat in peace now?" I and Merak both nodded at him. I then tried to take a steamed potato, but then Merak snatched it from my fork. I just rolled my eyes and took another one. I can't believe how childish he is. I tried to ignore him, but he then stood up and 'accidentally' hit my glass filled with water, and it got on my dress. He then said, "Oops! My bad. Sometimes my hand has a reflex of spilling water on people who deserve it." I couldn't resist a smile.

Then, I threw a potato at him, and so the food war had begun. We threw whatever was on the table and tried to dodge it as much as we could. The king just sat there, head palming at our childish behavior. After the king had enough, he shouted, "OK, that's enough dinner for the both of you! Get back to your rooms now!" Did I just get grounded by someone who isn't my father? I and Merak walked out of the now very filthy dinner room and both of us couldn't stop laughing at how childish we are.

Before I headed back to my room, he said, "Hey, how about a truce, no more 'accidents,' OK?" I held out my hand, and we shook hands. His hands were bigger than mine and very warm. He then left to get changed. I went to my room, took a shower under the little waterfall inside my room, and wore my normal clothes. Oh, how good it felt to wear my jeans again. I laid on the cozy bed and wondered when I could go back home, not that I wasn't happy.

I just wanted to make sure Atles knew I was OK. I then remembered my bracelet device. I quickly took it out of my little bag I had with me, and I saw that he called multiple times. Damn it! He must be worried sick. I quickly called him; he accepted the call and, just as I thought, he was worried. I then explained everything to him, and told him that I was fine, and he didn't need to worry.

Right after I ended the call, Merak barged in my room without knocking. How dare he? What if I was still naked? He really needs to learn a thing or two about manners. He looked at my bracelet device and said, "So, you're talking with the Komitaz?" I nodded. He said, "Why are you so obsessed with those Komitaz freaks? They wanted to attack Earth." I answered him and said, "Yea, well only because their kind were trapped here and getting tortured, I had to be on their side to save my own kind and save Earth." He was quiet for a few seconds, trying to think what he should say. He then looked at me with a serious look and said, "I'm sorry that you got kidnapped. I was annoyed that the humans are discriminating against us and destroying our Earth with their pathetic lifestyles. I never wanted to see any living being from Planet Earth get killed or hurt." I smiled and happily forgave him, and he was surprised that I did that so fast. I then said, "The sooner we forgive and forget, the sooner we can live in a better and more peaceful future." He gently smiled; it was the first time I saw him smile like that.

Then, he asked me to follow him. I didn't have anything better to do in this room, so I followed him. He brought me to large room with a huge, colorful strange precious rock. There was light emanating from it. Merak then said, "This is the Wikva. We are alive because of it; the Wikva gives us life energy … it's also the source of our magical abilities. Without it, we Kultraz would all die out." I wanted to touch it but resisted. Merak saw this, and he gently grabbed my hand and put it on the Wikva. It was very warm, and it felt so alive. I could feel a heartbeat inside it.

There was so much to learn from this place. I decided to stay here a little longer and learn as much as I could from them. Luckily, the king agreed to it and let me stay as long as I desired. I then called Sara, my boss from work, and told her that I won't be able to come to work because of some family business. I also called Atles and told him that I would stay here. He didn't like the idea, but since he knew I was too stubborn to listen, he just told me to be careful and said that he was going back to Planet Komitaz. I felt bad for just letting him leave like that, but I needed to know more about this island and this ancient race.

During the night, I quietly went back to the room where the Wikva was. No matter how long I looked at it, I couldn't stop staring at its beauty and mysterious appearance. I got out my sketch book and pencil and started sketching the Wikva.

I am really quite excited to explore this newfound island and see new things to draw.

CHAPTER 7

Conflict

These past weeks have been going great. Merak showed me all around the island. I saw and met a lot of animals that the rest of Earth thought died out thousands of years ago but were right here in front of my eyes. I even saw a T-Rex. They weren't as aggressive as they have been portrayed in dinosaur movies.

Merak has been genuinely nice to me. He introduced me to his friends and would always stay close to me, in case I get into trouble or danger. The island was not a very safe place; it was filled with dangerous animals and Kultraz, who are not very fond humans ... which is quite understandable if you ask me.

Merak and I were just walking around the jungle, when we stumbled into Ikaza again. She was plucking red apples from a tree and putting them in a basket. I greeted her and apologized for what happened back with Atles. She didn't say anything, so I asked her if she wanted to have a sleepover. She didn't seem to know what it was since she looked at me with a confused face. After I explained it to her, she hesitantly agreed.

Merak just dramatically rolled his eyes at us. I then turned to him and said, "You're just jealous that you're not invited." He chuckled and then told me to follow him back since it was getting late. I followed him together with Ikaza.

I let Ikaza in my room. I then gave her one of the dresses that were given to me by the king. She let me brush her hair and, while I was brushing her hair, the same question popped in my mind that I had back when she saved me from the kidnapper. Why doesn't she have wings like the rest of the Kultraz? I hesitated but my curiosity got the best of me, so I asked her. She didn't say anything. Then, I said, "I'm sorry. I shouldn't have asked." She then spoke and said, "My wings were taken from me ... by you humans." My eyes widened. Who could do such a thing? I then asked her, "Then why did you save me? I'm a human, too." She said, "You human saved me. I only save you human back." The rest of the night we didn't speak. I told her that, in a sleepover, you're supposed to also sleep over but, she refused to do so and left. I guess I shouldn't have asked her that. Maybe I reminded her of those bad memories again. I felt bad for her. The world is a terrible place where terrible things happen. I just wish that someday we could all live in peace and harmony together and accept each other no matter how we look or where we came from. But that's just a fantasy, nothing more.

The Next Day

I was walking around the castle looking for Merak. He promised me he would take me on another adventure on the island.

Strange. I looked everywhere. He was nowhere to be found. I ran out of patience. So, I put on my invisible ring, in case I needed to be invisible, and flew with my flying shoe soles alone. The island was so beautiful. It was colorful, and everywhere were all kinds of vegetation growing.

The Kultraz lived in a nature-friendly way. To them, everything that lives deserved to stay where it is. They didn't cut down trees. To them, the trees were holy because they gave them oxygen and food. Too bad humans don't see trees like that. They are also vegetarians. They don't eat animals because they see animals and everything else that was born on Earth, as their own equals. To them, everything that lives deserved to be protected and treated with respect and love.

They had a name for every tree, every rock, and every creature they met. Everything deserved to be treated with respect, no matter how they looked or what they were. It was a beautiful place. I wish the rest of Earth would also be like this, but that's a dream many wanted but failed trying. No matter what we do, discrimination and racism always exists. If only people would see how beautiful the world would be if we all treated each other equally and if we all did our best to prevent climate change and help the Earth recover. We could live in a colorful and magical world.

Just then a figure jumped and scared me from behind. I let out a loud scream. I quickly turned over to see what that was. It was Merak. He laughed and said, "That's what you get for going out without me." I playfully slapped his arm and said, "You jerk. I almost had a heart attack ... and besides, I looked for you, but you were nowhere to be found, so I left." He then said that he was with his father discussing something. When I asked what they talked about, he looked at me and playfully said, "I'm not telling you." He then stuck out his tongue. "'Ugh." He really is a kid. I rolled my eyes at him. He just chuckled.

We then landed on the coast and watched the beautiful blue sea. We could hear birds flying around freely. I then saw a bird, that was outside the barrier, easily came inside the island area. I then asked, "Why are the birds capable of coming here despite the barrier around this island?" Merak then replied, "Well, this barrier is not a shield. It only makes our island invisible. Anything or anyone could come here, but that never happens because this island is extremely far away from your human lands." I nodded in understanding. I breathed in the fresh air and said, "This place is beautiful. You all are right in trying to hide it. We humans would only destroy something so beautiful." He looked at me and said, "Not all humans ... I have met one good human who would never do such a thing." I looked at him, confused. He laughed and said,

"I mean you, you dummy." I laughed too. He really changed; he used to be a small-minded scary idiot, but now he is still an idiot but a kind one. I softly giggled to myself. He really was turning sweet though. I can't believe that I used to be scared of him. He looked at me and said, "What's so funny?" I told him that it was nothing, he looked at me irritated. I smiled at him; he really was a child even though he is much older than me. The Kultraz have a longer lifespan, also meaning that they age much slower than humans.

We then turned to each other and got lost in our gazes. I couldn't stop staring at his beautiful crimson eyes. He looked at me in a gentle and caring way. It made my heart speed up.

Then, something in the distance grabbed my attention. I looked behind Merak and saw a man pointing a shotgun at us. I shouted, "LOOK Out!!" But the second Merak wanted to look behind him, he got shot. A painfully forced grunt came out of him, and he fell on the beach. I stood in front of him trying to guard him from the stranger.

The man then ran toward me and pointed the gun at me. I closed my eyes ready to feel the pain, but when I heard another gun shot, I didn't feel anything. I opened my eyes and saw Merak standing in front of me. He caught the bullet for me. He protectively put his wings around me. I felt the tears coming out of my eyes. Why is this happening?

When the man was about to reload his gun, Merak flew toward him and, with one punch to the stomach, he threw the man on the other side of the beach. Merak then broke the gun with his bare hands and fell to the ground. I quickly ran to catch him even though he was so heavy. He lost consciousness, but he was still breathing. Thank god. I cried out for help and, after a couple of seconds, a random Kultraz landed on the beach next to us. I quickly told him to take Merak to a healer. He did what I said and flew off while carrying Merak on his back. I then walked up to the man who shot Merak. He was also still alive. I took the mini gun he had in his pocket and pointed it at him. The man slowly opened his eyes and looked at me. I then said, "Tell me how you got here and who sent you, or else I will not hesitate to shoot." He laughed and said, "A little girl like you won't scare me."

I then thought about Merak, who is literally fighting for his life right now and felt the anger rising in me. So, without thinking, I shot one of the man's legs. He loudly grunted in pain. I then repeated myself. When he still didn't say anything, I stepped on his leg where I shot it. He then quickly said, "I work for Dr. Brandon. We were sent to kidnap you, but when you somehow got away after we sent someone for you, we started following you. And when you went through the portal, we used the signal of your phone to track where you went." I couldn't believe it. This was all my fault. Merak is hurt because of me. I see that Dr. Brandon is still out for revenge for what I did. That guy doesn't know when to quit.

Two Kultraz warriors came flying by and landed on the beach. They then carried the man to the castle to put him in the dungeon for attacking their prince. I followed them to the castle to see how Merak was doing. I went inside the healers' room and saw that Merak was naked in a pool with clear water. There were three healers surrounding him and saying things in their own language. The water started to shine, and I saw the bullets coming out of Merak and floating in the water.

I wanted to go to him but felt guilty. It was all my fault that this happened to him. I turned around and went to the thrones room, only to see the man there being interrogated by the king. I quietly entered the room and heard him say, "You monsters are going to pay very soon. I have already sent the signal to my boss. Soon, this island will be surrounded by a huge army. and it's all thanks to her." He pointed at me while saying the last bit. Then he started laughing like the maniac he was. King Kurek and the rest of the Kultraz looked at me, trying to figure out if the man was telling the truth.

The king then ordered the man to be put inside their dungeon and ended the meeting. What am I supposed to do? This was a mess. This place was about to turn into a war zone – because of me. Now, all the Kultraz probably think that I really betrayed them.

I went to my room and started thinking of what I should do. Coco then came on my bed and cuddled himself on my lap, I put my hand on his head and petted him gently. While I was busy in my thoughts. I then took out my communication device I got from Planet Komitaz and contacted the leader of the Komitaz. When I heard the leader say, "Hello, who is this?" I quickly told him it was me and asked him if he could help us from this unpleasant situation. He didn't say anything for a couple of seconds trying to think of what he should do. I just sat on my bed waiting in suspense for what he would answer, while feeling a little hope rise. He then said, "I'm sorry Tayler, but I will not risk the lives of my people to help the very race that never wanted to form a bond with us. After all, they saw us as outsiders and wanted to have nothing to do with us." He then ended the call without letting me say anything. I just sat there, feeling hopeless and pathetic, I guess this time I can't prevent war from happening. Coco then jumped off of me and waited in front of the door. The door then opened, and it was Merak. He was topless. I looked at his body and saw the places where he got shot. He grabbed Coco and put him around his arms and walked over to me and sat on the bed while stifling a grunt. He must still be in pain ... all thanks to me. My stomach turned because of all the guilt I was feeling.

I looked at him with guilt and said, "I'm sorry. It's because of me you're hurt." He looked at me with a confused look, and I then said, "The man found this place because of me. They tracked my phone signal. This is all my fault. I shouldn't have come here." He stared at me trying to process what I just said. Just when I thought he was going to get angry at me, he gently held my hand and said, "This is not your fault. Since the moment I met you, I saw what a good person you really were. You always try to help everyone around you, without thinking of the risks it may have for you ... your kindness awakened something in me that I didn't know I had." He squeezed my hands a little and continued, "It was you who made me fall in love with the only race I hated since the moment I knew of their existence ... and as much as I tried to prevent this feeling, I still ended up falling for this human." We gazed into each other's eyes. I looked at his beautiful red crimson eyes. I felt like I could get lost in them forever. We stood there staring at each other, it felt like time had stopped. I felt a nice sensation in my stomach. My heart skipped a beat when he gently put his warm hand on my cheek. He moved closer to me. I closed my eyes, ready to feel his lips on mine, but then the reality hit me again. This wasn't the right time for this. There was war coming, and whether it is or is not my fault, I still felt that it was. So, I opened my eyes and moved away from him before he could get any closer. I then apologized again, stood up and left the room, leaving him there.

I'm sorry, Merak, but there is something more important I had to do.

I called Atles and demanded that he would come and pick me up. Without questioning me, he traveled back to Earth, and, thanks to the signal of my communicator, he knew where to find me. I got on his ship and told him to take me to Planet Komitaz. When I was on the ship, I saw Merak standing outside looking at me. I suddenly realized I never even thanked him for protecting me. I'm such a horrible person. Atles looked at me waiting for me to give the signal for if he should go or not. I looked at Merak and got off the ship and walked up to him. He looked at me without saying anything. I then said to him, "Come with me and help me convince the Komitaz to help your people. I know that you all have had your differences with the Komitaz, but you also know that the Komitaz are the only ones who can help." He looked at me and then at Atles, who was still in his ship, and then he said, "I can't, I must stay here and protect my people, will you not stay here with me?" I then said, "I will come back, but I need to do this first." When I realized that he wasn't coming with us, I then thanked him for saving me and turned toward the ship. Then I felt him wrap his arms around me from behind, and he whispered in my ear with his husky voice, "You better come back to me; I'm not done with you, human." I felt my stomach flutter, like there were butterflies in me. I tried to ignore this nice feeling and focus on the war that was coming. Just by holding me I could feel how strong he is. I somehow felt safe with him and a part of me wanted to stay in his safe embrace. Once he let go, I turned around to look at him. I didn't know what to say to him, so I quickly went back inside the spaceship and asked Atles to go.

Help?

On the way to Komitaz, Atles was quiet. Something I really appreciated because I was not in the mood to talk. I was really stressed out and completely lost in my thoughts. I was trying to figure out what I should do now. I know the Komitaz leader already rejected me, but I had to try one more time to convince him.

When we finally landed on Komitaz, we headed straight to the main building. The Komitaz all looked at me surprised to see me once again. I headed to the room where the leader was sitting on his throne. A bunch of Komitaz got curious and came in the room. The leader looked at me, shocked to see me here. I then said, "I know what you said, but just so you know, you are in my debt ... I risked my life to save your kind, and now I'm asking you to do the same with my friends." I breathed in and out and continued. "I'm asking you all to set your differences aside with the Kultraz race and help me end this upcoming war and prevent unnecessary lives from being taken." The leader looked at me with a dead serious face and answered, "We are not in your debt. The only reason you saved our kind was to save your own home. You didn't do anything for us. Even without you, we would have been able to act and defeat your race and bring our kind back." He then turned to Atles and continued, "... now, Commander Atles, take her back home." I just stood there shocked by how he acted toward me. I didn't understand. I helped them once. Why won't they just help me? I dropped to the ground, closed my eyes, feeling the tears coming out. I felt like I was sinking in the ground. Atles tried to help me up and take me back to the ship, but then I heard a familiar voice shout out, "I will help!!!" I looked to where the voice came from. It was Maver. He walked up to me and lent me his hand to help me up. I stood up, and he said, "I will come to Earth and help you. After all, it's because of you that my daughter came back to me." I then heard another familiar voice shout out, "We will also help you, my heroine!!" I looked over and, just as I thought, it was Aton and behind him were the five Komitaz I rescued back at Area 51. I felt the hope rising around me. Then a bunch of other random Komitaz also said that they would help me. I couldn't resist a smile. I wiped the drops of tears that rolled down my face with the sleeve of my shirt. Atles put his hand on my shoulder and looked at me with a proud smile. The leader sighed and said, "Very well, if you all want to save the Kultraz and help the human girl, then very much do so." He then looked at me and gave me his gun bracelet and said, "Take this with you. You might need it ... As always, your actions make us all do things we never thought of doing." I took it and thanked him.

We headed to Earth with five spaceships filled with armed Komitaz. I put on the bracelet gun and sat next to Atles. When I saw Planet Earth, I breathed in and out, trying to gather some courage. I never thought that I would be going into battle again. But this time it was different; I wasn't alone, and, because of that, I felt more at ease. We landed on the secret Kultraz island. The spaceship doors opened. I then got a little blinded by the light coming from outside. OK, I can do this; I did this before, so I can do it again. Atles grabbed my hand after seeing that I was a bit anxious. I smiled at him and walked out of the spaceship. I then flew to the castle while the army of all the Komitaz followed behind me.

I landed in front of the castle. The king must have known we were coming since he was there waiting for us together with Merak and a whole army of Kultraz behind them. I told the Komitaz to stay back and let me do the talking. They all nodded, and so I walked up to the king and said, "You don't need to worry, my king, they are here to help protect your home." He looked at me with a serious look and said, "Why should I trust outsiders? How do I know they are not here to take our riches?" I said, "No. I swear to you, my king, they only came here to help. I asked them to come. You can't win this fight alone. We humans may be weaker than your kind but, I have seen what my kind is capable of building. If the Komitaz don't help us, this place will cease to exist." That was all true. After what I had seen at Area 51, who knows what other dangerous weapons they will use to bring this place down and steal everything valuable on this island … like the rare animals that were supposed to have died long ago. I bet they would put these animals in zoos and make money from them. Merak looked at me. Then, he turned to the king and said, "We should trust her; she helped Earth once –" He was interrupted by the king who said, "Exactly. These outsiders were planning on destroying our Earth. How can I ever trust a race who threatened our dear home planet." We then heard a loud explosion on the other side of the island. They are here …

Merak shouted, "It's coming from the east coast!! Warriors, come with me!" He then flew to where the explosion was heard, together with the king and a whole army of Kultraz.

Atles and the rest of the Komitaz looked at me waiting for my orders. Wow, I never knew I would end up leading an actual army. I then said, "All of you follow them and please be careful." They all nodded and also flew toward the danger. I was about to follow the rest but was stopped by Atles, who ordered me to stay behind since this was getting too dangerous. How was this more dangerous than the time I had to fight a whole military on my own? He gave me a cold look and said, "I will not ask again. Last time, you were lucky to be alive. Besides, you have done more than enough. Now stay here, OK?" I looked down. I guess he was right. What am I trying to prove here. It doesn't matter what I do. I will always be the weak girl I've always been. I looked to the ground and nodded. Atles then turned around and followed the others to the battlefield, leaving me behind.

I was the only one left behind. I could hear screams, shouts, explosions, and gun shots from afar. It wasn't fair that they were all fighting for their lives, and I had to be here even though I could help. I couldn't take it anymore. I flew toward the war field, but while I was flying above the sky, I saw an airplane heading toward the castle, where the Wikva was.

The enemy is attacking in two fronts. I thought I should contact Atles and tell him to head here, but then I heard even more explosions coming from the east and figured that the Komitaz and the Kultraz had their hands full there. So, it was now up to me to help and make myself useful for once.

I flew on top of the plane, shot a hole on top of the plane with my bracelet, and went inside the ship. The pilot started shouting through his mic that he was in danger. I then saw a giant atomic bomb. I knew it, they were trying to destroy the whole island in one blow. My whole body trembled, and I felt my heart quickening.

I ran up to the pilot and aimed the bracelet gun at him and shouted, "YOU will listen to me now! Fly this plane somewhere far away from here and far away from every other land filled with innocent lives!! Or else I will not hesitate to kill you. I have already killed the one who discovered this island!!" Of course, I lied that I killed the man that shot Merak, but I had to seem as dangerous as possible. He didn't say anything and continued to fly the plane towards the castle where the Wikva was. If he destroyed the Wikva he would kill every Kultraz alive. He then said, "This is something a little girl like you would never understand. Now put the weapon down, stop this madness, and join your own race." I got angry and said, "How can I join my own race, if I see them trying to kill out an entire innocent race?" He then replied, "Innocent?! How are they innocent? Do you have any idea what they did to our race? All those people they kidnapped and killed? Who knows what else they might do in the future?" I then said, "We humans are also not innocent. We drove the Kultraz into hiding, and there are a couple of Kultraz I met that were once captured by humans and tortured. And let's not forget what you guys did to the Komitaz race." He looked like he was thinking, and I then said, "We are all guilty here. We all did bad things to each other, but we can't stop this by killing out an entire race ... If you do this, there will be a lot of bad consequences, so please do the right thing and help me stop this madness." He looked at me and seemed to be lost in his thoughts trying to process what I just said. He was reconsidering it. But then Barak, a Kultraz I met while exploring the island, appeared. He was blocking our view with his big wings; we couldn't see where we were flying. The pilot then set the auto pilot on in case we crashed onto something.

The past weeks on this island, Barak has always looked at me with his scary white eyes. He really hated humans. He was also the Kultraz who kidnapped me from the woods. Merak always would stand in front of me, guarding me from Barak. The way Barak was looking at us was not a good sign. He looked mad, as usual. He then used his magic to construct a giant axe and started smashing and destroying the plane.

I quickly shouted to the pilot, "Quickly, fly this plane to the sea. If the bomb falls like this, it will destroy the island with us in it!!" The pilot did what I said, and we headed out to the sea, far away from the island. I then quickly told the pilot to hold onto me. He did that, and we flew out of the plane before the plane – and bomb – crashed into the sea.

Darn, the pilot is so heavy. I quickly flew us back to the island, and then we heard the bomb go off, just as I thought. Even on the island, we could still feel the explosion the bomb made. The explosion of the bomb wasn't very powerful, thanks to the sea, which helped lessen the impact of the explosion.

We were both panting and catching our breath after surviving death. I didn't see Barak. I'm glad he is out of sight; this isn't the time to be dealing with him. The pilot looked at me and said, "You saved my life. I would have been dead without you." I didn't say anything. This wasn't the time for pathetic talking. I needed to help the others now, but then he continued, "My name is Tom Redford, and, after what you did, I want to help you as much as I can." I then said, "Just tell me where your leader is." He nodded. To win and stop a war, you must always go for the leader. That is something I learned from chess. He told me that the leader's name was General Callaway and that he is helping Dr. Brandon with this mission to eliminate all the Kultraz on Earth. Tom also said that it was Dr. Brandon who found out that the Wikva was the key to destroying the entire Kultraz race. Seriously, that scientist just doesn't know when to give up.

I then thanked him for helping me and flew toward to the east coast.

While I was flying, I then felt a powerful and painful weight on my back and fell from the sky. Everything went dark for a couple of seconds. When I came back to my senses, I saw that it was Barak. He kicked me out of the sky.

That idiot! I could have died from a fall from that height. I somehow survived thanks to a tree, which broke my fall. I then felt pain all over my body. I just sat there trying to endure the pain. Barak then said in a deep voice, "You are the reason this is all happening. I knew keeping you around here would bring our home and people in danger" I just looked at him and felt the tears forcing their way out of my eyes. I tried to keep them in, but it was no use, they started rolling out of my eyes. Then, he constructed a blade with his magic. He slowly walked to where I was and said, "I can finally kill you now. You know, the second I kidnapped you from the woods, I wanted to see you die, and now I can finally see it done." My whole body felt heavy; I couldn't stand up because of the pain, I couldn't even move. He came closer to me. I felt so hopeless; I just gave up. He was in front of me now and raised his blade at me, ready to slice my head off. He then whispered, "Now you will die, filthy human." I then closed my eyes, ready to feel more pain.

Suddenly I heard a loud gunshot. I opened my eyes and saw that Barak was shot and fell to the ground. Behind him, I saw Dr. Brandon pointing his gun at him. I looked at him, shocked to see him, of all people. He looked at me seriously and tried to walk away, but then Barak quickly stood up and flew toward him, the blade piercing right through Dr. Brandon. I couldn't believe my eyes; I held my hand on my mouth in disbelief. Barak shouted, "YOU FILTHY HUMANS THINK YOU CAN KILL ME THAT EASILY?!" He then turned toward me and said, "I guess you really thought you got rid of me. Well, too bad, because it's your turn!!"

I then felt the energy rising inside me. I stood up, aimed my bracelet at him and shot him dead. I ran up to Dr. Brandon, who was still alive and spitting out blood. I squatted next to him and said, "Why did you do that? Why did you save me after what I did to you?" He looked at me and said, "All I wanted was to find a way to protect the human race from all those powerful and dangerous races among us ... you were never my enemy, little girl." He then closed his eyes and was out. I checked his pulse to see if he really was dead this time. After I checked, I felt that he had no pulse …

He died thinking that what he did was right. I felt the tears coming out again. I then realized that all this time I saw the humans as the enemies, but now I see that there is no enemy. Everyone does what they think is right to them. Everyone thinks they're the good guy in their own point of view. What can I do to end this war and make them see that we can all become allies instead of enemies?

Atles Perspective

We landed on the eastern coast and saw the enormous number of humans come out of the boats. They all attacked, and we did the same. The Kultraz used their magic to construct weapons and used them to drive the humans away. I told the Komitaz to all stick with each other and be careful. I saw a human aiming his gun at the Kultraz, who took Tayler to this island. His name was Merak. That's the name I heard Tayler call him by. I shot the human before he could try anything. Merak then turned toward me and nodded his head once, to show his thanks. I nodded back at him and continued killing as much soldiers as I could. The smell of death was in the air. Everywhere I looked were dead bodies.

I then saw Aton get shot multiple times. He fell to the ground in pain. I ran toward him, squatted next to him. I analyzed his injuries. He was losing too much blood. He wasn't going to survive this. Aton looked at my reaction then said, "I know that it's the end for me. Please take good care of Tayler. She is a good girl and deserves to have a peaceful life here on Earth." He closed his eyes and took his last breath. To think that he had to endure so much pain by the humans back when he was captured for years in Area 51, and now, he ended up getting killed anyway. This must stop; all this killing isn't going anywhere. I looked around me and saw how barbarically everyone was killing each other. I need to find Tayler and find a way to stop this together with her.

I flew away from all the chaos around me and went back to the place I left her.

When I landed in front of the castle, she was nowhere to be seen. I checked my bracelet device to see where she was. I then followed the signal to find her.

Tayler Perspective

I was walking through the forest, hearing the war play out on the other side of the island and acting like it was the most normal thing. I used to watch several war movies, and I never would have thought that I would be in a war one day.

I heard footsteps coming toward me, I quickly aimed my bracelet gun at the unknown person approaching me and said, "Who is there? Show yourself!" The unknown person slowly came to me, and I felt so relieved to see him. I ran up to him and hugged him. Atles hugged me back and said, "What are you doing all the way over here? I thought I told you to stay at the castle." I broke the hug and said, "It's a long story. I will tell you later." He looked at me curiously. I told him that we needed to go find General Callaway, who is leading this war. We first headed to the castle where I grabbed my X-ray glasses from my little bag.

Then, we flew to the war field and stayed above in the sky while people were killing each other below us. I tried to ignore everything and focus. I put my glasses on and looked at the war ships. I saw a lot of soldiers still in there waiting to attack. I then saw three figures far away from the rest of the soldiers in a room above the biggest ship that laid in the middle between the two other ships. That had to be him, I told Atles. So, we used our rings to make ourselves invisible and headed there.

We got into the main ship without being noticed. We quietly headed to the room where we saw the three figures standing. We stood in front of the door and could hear shouts and laughter coming out of the room. We made ourselves visible again and, on Atles's signal, we stormed into the room. The second the men wanted to shoot us, I shot one of the man's legs while Atles shot the other man's leg. After that, we both aimed our bracelet gun at the third man, who raised his hands in defeat. I then said, "Are you General Callaway?" He nodded, and I smiled at Atles and said, "You are coming with us, and you will help us stop this meaningless war." He nodded in defeat. I felt a bit lightheaded; I never thought it would be that easy. We only needed to show the soldiers out there that we got their leader, and they will all also surrender. Atles grabbed the general, but once we turned our backs, I saw one of the men lying on the ground grab their gun. He quickly aimed at Atles, but the second he shot, I stood in front of Atles and felt the sharp stabbing familiar pain. I fell to the ground. Atles turned around and shot the man, killing him immediately. General Callaway ran away after seeing an opening. I told Atles to follow him, but instead of doing that, he came to me and carried me bridal style while I was screaming in pain. The pain was too much this time. I looked at where the pain was coming from. It was my chest. My head was spinning, and I heard Atles talking to me, but I couldn't understand anything, I only heard a peeping noise surrounding my ears. Then, I couldn't feel my body anymore. And, before I could do anything, it all went black ...

Merak Perspective

I was fighting off and killing every human I faced. If I never met Tayler, I would have enjoyed this, but ever since I have feelings for her, I have been seeing humans in a different way.

My picture of the human race suddenly changed. That girl really is something; no one has ever been able to change me so quick. I then could smell her scent nearby. I looked around but didn't see her. Then, I saw her and saw the Komitaz with her. His name is Atles, I heard Tayler call him that when she called him the other time with her device. He also saved me earlier. They went into the main ship, while using their Komitaz technology to be invisible. Thanks to our magic, we Kultraz can see everything that is invisible to human eyes. We can even see the signals the humans use to communicate with each other.

Then, I followed Tayler and Atles. I had to fight once I was on the ship and used my magic to construct a shield to protect myself from gunshots. I then saw a man with a different kind of suit than the other human running my way. I analyzed him and knew that he was the leader of the humans. I quickly grabbed him before he could do anything and shouted, "Where is the girl?!" He pointed at the room all the way down the hall. I dragged him with me to where Tayler was. When I opened the door and saw Tayler unconscious in Atles's arms, I felt my heart weakening. She was covered in her blood. Atles looked at me, and I threw the human leader into the room and said, "You better stay right there. Make one move and you're dead!" I then asked Atles what happened. After he explained it to me, I felt the anger rising. Why does she always have to do stupid stuff without thinking about it? I felt drops of liquid coming down my face and I realized I was crying. Who would have thought a prideful Kultraz prince like me would be crying because of a human girl? I took Tayler from Atles, who wanted to protest, but then I said, "I will take her to the healers." He then nodded and let me take her. I carefully carried her bridal style and flew as fast as I could toward the castle, where the healers were. I carefully set her inside the sacred pool, where the healers use their magic to heal all the wounded on this island.

The healers told me that it would take long because she was not strong and had lost too much blood already. I wish I could have stayed here with her, but there was a war that had to be stopped.

After I headed back to the war field, Atles and I held the human leader and stood somewhere high for everyone to see. I shouted, "HUMANS, WE HAVE YOUR LEADER. IF YOU DON'T ALL SURRENDER, WE WILL KILL HIM!!" It didn't take long before they all raised their hands in defeat and put down their arms. The Kultraz all shouted and screamed in happiness, while the Komitaz looked relieved. The war was finally over.

After A Couple Of Hours

I and my father went to the coast where the Komitaz had landed their spaceships. Atles told the Komitaz to head back to Planet Komitaz without him. We then walked up to them, and my father then said, "We thank you all for helping us. Without you, we would have lost more lives than we have lost now." I then said, "We stand in your debt." Atles then said, "Don't thank us. We came here only for Tayler. She is the one you should be thanking." The king looked at me, and I nodded. The king then said, "I know that this took a very long time to do, but we would like to reconsider your proposal that your kind discussed with our kind ..." Atles looked at him, trying to figure out what he wanted to say. The king then continued, "After your kindness toward our race, you have proven your loyalty to us. Therefore, we would like to start a friendship and alliance between our races, if that is still possible." Atles then said, "We will inform our leader." Then, all the Komitaz went inside their spaceships, excluding Atles, and left. We headed back to the castle with Atles following us. While the king went to fulfill his duties as the king, I and Atles went to the healers' room to see if Tayler is awake now.

We quietly went inside the room and saw her in the pool. She was still unconscious, and I saw that she was wearing only her undergarments. I saw where she was shot. It looked bad. I looked over to Atles, who looked at her with guilt and pain in his eyes. He then said, "This is not the first time that I see her like that ... in pain and unconscious. She always risks her own life to save and help others around her." We then left the room to let the healers do their job properly. And we hoped she would soon wake up in good health.

CHAPTER 8

Dead Or Alive?

A whole week passed by, and Tayler was still unconscious. Atles was still here, determined to stay here until she woke up. Everyone else lost the hope and thought that it was over for her. Since it is said that if the mighty Kultraz healers couldn't help someone wake up after a week, the chances of the person not coming back would be very large. Atles and I were the only ones keeping the hope alive. We were the only ones who knew how strong she really is. She had to fight back, she just had to.

The king had organized a worthy funeral for every Kultraz, Komitaz and animal that died during the war. As for the leader of the humans, he signed a truce and promised to leave the Kultraz island alone and to tell no one about our existence. We won the war and put them all in their place. We also signed a form to prove to them that we Kultraz would never threaten or come near the human race ever again. Therefore, Planet Earth would be in peace – no one ever believed that was possible. Every race was living in their own land in peace. It's not really the kind of peace Tayler wished for all of us, but it's for the best. We accept the fact that our differences can't be accepted in human society. But maybe in the future, things could change. Who knows? Maybe, one day, the Kultraz and the humans would all live together in acceptance and peace.

I went inside the room and saw that the healers were done. They all turned to me and bowed. One of the healers then said, "We did all we could. Now, it is up to her to fight back." I nodded, and they all left the room. I squatted next to her, gently stroked her cheek with my hand and whispered to her to not give up and to keep fighting for her life. She still didn't make a noise or even move; but I could see her chest slowly rising up and down with her breathing. I gently kissed her forehead and left her alone in the room.

My heart was in pain, seeing her every day get a little paler and weaker. I went to the room that she stayed in and saw her little bag she had with her when I took her here. I looked inside it and took out a little book and leafed through it. I saw the beautiful sketches she made. She had made a lot of sketches of this place and of the animals here. I then stopped at a drawing that looked like me. She had sketched me. I smiled while holding in the tears and pictured how I would have teased her about it and made her blush in embarrassment. Gosh, how I missed her. I would do anything to see her beautiful lively face flush red again. Coco then suddenly appeared and cuddled on my lap, I put the little book back inside her bag and carried Coco with me out of the room.

Atles Perspective

I still couldn't believe it. One second she was with me, so alive and well. Then, the next second, she was on the ground looking pale and lifeless. I couldn't stop picturing the moment she closed her eyes and fell unconscious in my arms. It was all my fault; if only I didn't drop my guard, she would have still been here. I feel so pathetic. Since the moment I met her, she has done nothing more than help me in every way possible. Without her, I would have still been on Earth, stuck in the woods with no food. I always wished I could once help her, the way she helped me. But instead of helping her, I only brought her into more danger and pain. Seeing her in the pool looking so pale broke my heart. I heard everyone talking about how hopeless it was for her and that she would not wake up anymore. That only made me feel worse, but I never let myself lose all hope. I had to still believe in her. It's the least I can do.

My leader contacted me and told me that they needed me for a mission. They had discovered a new planet with strange life forms, and they needed me to investigate it. But I ignored his orders and said that I needed to be here with Tayler. If I leave Earth, it will also mean that I had lost hope for Tayler to awaken.

Unexpected Adventure

Tayler POV

I could hear everything happening around me and feel everything. No matter what I did, I just couldn't wake up. I felt like I was in a nightmare, where I couldn't talk or move.

Atles was right about me. I was lucky when I survived Area 51. I didn't want to believe it and felt like I could be useful for once. But all that brought me to this. I couldn't even die in peace; I was somewhere between life and death.

Every day, I felt like I was moving toward the side of death. Every day, the restful feeling of death would try to devour me and push me to its side. But every time I heard Merak's and Atles's voices next to me, it gave me the motivation to fight back and run back to the side of life.

I tried hard to wake up and keep fighting to stay on the side of life. But I felt weaker by the day, and I could see the side of death growing larger each time.

I missed my family, my parents, Anne, and, of course, Atles and Merak. I didn't even want to know what they would do if I lost this fight. I didn't want them to cry for me. After all, the adventures I had and the places I went to were more than enough fun. I loved every moment of my life. I do wish I had a chance to say goodbye to everyone, but I felt that my time had come. I felt my body weakening, and the side of death overwhelmed me. I was so tired of resisting it; I finally gave up and proceeded to walk through the dark bridge of death.

Then, suddenly I saw a beautiful white light, lighting up the whole dark place. I then heard a voice say, "Your time is not now."

I opened my eyes and stood up. I can't believe it! I'm finally awake. I then saw that I was wearing only my undergarments. Oh my god. Don't tell me everyone saw me like this. This is so embarrassing. Now I think I preferred to have died and not have to know this. I'm just kidding, of course. I was more than happy to be alive. I felt stronger and more alive than before. I couldn't wait to see everyone again, but first I had to put on more clothes. The door of the room suddenly opened, and there stood Atles and Merak looking at me, as if I was a ghost or something. Before they could come closer, I shouted, "Stay away from me! And stop looking at me, you perverts!" They were shocked by my reaction, but also looked relieved that I had finally woken up. Atles smiled and looked away in respect, but Merak smirked at me and said, "Well, just so you know, when you were still unconscious, I had a good amount of time to check you all out." He then laughed. I felt the anger rising. That jerk! I wanted to kick him so badly now, but then I sighed in relief and felt so grateful to be here with them again, to be alive.

I then went to my room to put on some more clothes. Atles and Merak followed me close. I guess I made them really worried about me. It's like they don't want to leave my side anymore. I am glad everything turned out well. But I'm not sure if I can go back to my normal life anymore. I don't even think I can be normal anymore ... or want to be normal again.

After I was fully dressed, I then said, "OK, you guys can hug me now." They smiled and hugged me tightly. When we parted, Atles said that he had to go now. I looked at him with disbelief and asked why. He then explained that he needed to go back since the Komitaz had made an incredible discovery of new life on a new planet they found.

I got curious; I wonder what the new life forms looked like. Atles looked at me with a smile. Then asked me if I wanted to go with him. I looked at Merak, who stared right at me, wondering what I would say. I then turned to Atles, who patiently waited for my response, and I then said, "I don't think I want to go back to my normal life again. I guess I might as well go with you then." Atles smiled and nodded. Merak then looked at Atles and said, "Well, in that case, I'm coming too. Someone has to keep an eye on this human." I rolled my eyes at him. Merak then ruffled my hair gently. Atles then agreed to take him too, and we all went to pack our stuff to leave. Merak carried me bridal style and flew me all the way to my apartment to get new clothes and food supplies.

While I was looking for the things I might need for this adventure, I saw my goldfish floating lifelessly upside down in the water. Oops, I forgot all about him. This was the reason why I should never have pets; I am not responsible enough to take care of them. I flushed the fish in the toilet and told him to rest in peace, while Merak dramatically shook his head and said, "You should not be allowed to take care of living beings anymore. You basically can't even take care of yourself." I turned to him and said, "Hey, what do you mean by that!?" He walked to the living room, and I followed him. He then pointed at all the mess. I guess he was kind of right. I then said, "I didn't have time to clean everything. Besides, even if I clean it, it will just get messy again." He laughed, then gently looked at me with his beautiful crimson eyes. He cupped my face with his big warm hands, squeezing my face gently. He then put his arms around me and took me in his warm, safe embrace. I felt my heart speeding up. I then realized that he hasn't left my side since I woke up. Even back when I was still in coma, I could hear him coming to check on me every day for hours. He then said in his low husky voice, "I can feel your heart beating faster … am I making you nervous, human?" I felt the heat reaching my cheeks. I bet my face was flushed red now. I quickly pushed him away, went to the bathroom, and locked it. I relaxed my breathing and felt my heart relaxing. I then washed my face, with freezing water to cool off my heated face. Why do I always feel so nervous and excited when he teases me like that? I can't even control my own body.

It's like he holds the strings to control me.

He makes me feel these strange emotions, and I then remembered that he basically confessed to me, before I left to Planet Komitaz. Back then, I didn't answer him because of the war. I guess he must still be waiting for my response then. To be honest I still didn't know what I felt for him or even what I felt for Atles. They basically both make me nervous when they come a little too close to me.

Oh well, this isn't the time to think about this. When the day comes to confront this feeling, I will hopefully know what to do. For now, I needed to get ready. I was going on a new fun adventure. So, no stress and just have fun. I deserve the fun after what I went through.

I then called my parents and told them that I was going on a long vacation with a couple of good friends. They told me to have fun and be careful. It was nice to hear their voices again, but I wish I could tell them what I'm actually doing and just tell them the truth for once. Oh well, when the time comes, I think I would tell them everything that happened and is still happening. But for now, I don't want them to get tangled in this. I also told Sara, my boss, from work to just fire me since I haven't worked there for so long. Sara was a little frustrated that I quit over a phone call instead of coming to see her personally. If only she knew what I went through, she wouldn't be complaining and should be grateful that I at least called her. Whatever. I am not letting anyone disturb my hard-won fun.

Atles picked us up, with his spaceship, and we finally took off. So, I guess this is how my life will be then. No more normal. I'll just roll with the weirdness and action around me.

Besides after I almost died, I realized that life is too short to be living a long boring normal life. I might as well make the most of every single moment I still have.

The author

Talar S. Mohammed was born and lives in the
Netherlands. She enjoys, drawing, reading and
watching fantasy movies. Using her creativity, she
wrote this book. As this is her first publication, she
hopes to have a successful career as an author.